Happy
Endings

Adèle Geras
Happy Endings

Harcourt Brace Jovanovich, Publishers

SAN DIEGO   NEW YORK   LONDON

First published 1986 by Hamish Hamilton Children's Books, London
Copyright © 1986 by Adèle Geras

Permission was granted to print passages from *Three Sisters*,
by Anton Chekhov, translated by Michael Frayn.
Reprinted from *Plays* by permission of
Michael Frayn and Methuen Books, London.
Copyright © 1983 by Michael Frayn.

Library of Congress Cataloging-in-Publication Data
Geras, Adèle.
Happy Endings/Adèle Geras.—1st U.S. ed.
p. cm.
Summary: Sixteen-year-old Mel encounters a tangled web of relationships
and her first romance when she is cast in a local theater company's
production of "Three Sisters."
ISBN 0-15-233375-4
[1. Theater—Fiction.] I. Title.
PZ7.G29354Hap 1991 90-46031
[Fic]—dc20

Printed in the United States of America

First United States edition

A B C D E

Author's Note

I would like to thank all the people in Manchester's theaters who helped me during the time that I was working on this novel:

From the Royal Exchange Theatre—Sophie Marshall, Braham Murray, Moss Cooper, Jackie Morgan, Jimmy Booth, Geraldine Corrigan, and members of the cast (in alphabetical order) of Trevor Peacock's musical, *Class K*, Angie Deamer, Joanne Downs, Lisa Geoghan, Rosalind Knight, Crispin Letts, Elaine Lordan, Cyril Nri, and Sara Sugarman.

From the Contact Theatre—Barbara Pemberton.

From the Library Theatre—Josh Dynevor.

From the Palace Theatre—Nora Cullen, Geoff Joyce.

The theater in this book is not intended to be any of the above. I have devised a fictional one to suit the purposes of the story. Similarly, all the characters are products of my imagination.

I owe a debt of gratitude to Casper Wrede and the company of *Three Sisters* presented at the Royal Exchange in April 1985, in Michael Frayn's translation. This was a beautiful production which provided much of the inspiration for this book.

Special thanks to Michael Frayn for a memorable and illuminating lecture on Chekhov, given at the Royal Exchange on May 10th, 1985, and to him and Methuen, London, for permission to quote from his translation of the play.

Adèle Geras

After I broke my ankle, my mother moved my bed downstairs and the front room of our house became my private island. Visitors, even my mother, look out of place here. I'm used to being with most of them somewhere else, and it's amazing how the setting in which you're accustomed to seeing someone becomes a part of them, like an accessory to their dress.

Clare has just left. While she was here she sat on the red chair, looking polite, being much quieter than she normally is. Her hands lay still in her lap, without a pen or a pencil to occupy them, and the fact that she wasn't carrying anything except a parcel wrapped in pretty paper (which I hoped would turn out to be a present for me) was even more unsettling. My image of Clare is of someone hung about with papers of one kind or another: little pads, huge sheets of sugar paper rolled up and stuck under one arm,

1

graph paper crisscrossed with spider-lines of ink, all sorts—
you name it.

"It's really lovely here," she said. "What a good idea to
have the bed up by the window. You can see all the comings
and goings."

"I feel as if I'm marooned," I answered. "This is my
island. This lamp is a beacon, and at night it shines out
over dark water. Over there, where the carpet ends, there
are waves stretching to the horizon. My mother comes with
provisions in a little boat, and I get visitors, of course, also
in boats."

"What's my boat like, then?" Clare smiled. I liked the
fact that she didn't think I'd lost my reason entirely.

"Yours is a punt. You're moored outside my door under
a willow tree."

Clare laughed. She has dark hair cut into short spikes
and was dressed in wide black trousers and a denim jacket,
but still, there is about her a definite air of long dresses in
pale colors and wide-brimmed straw hats with roses tucked
into the satin headbands.

"You've got too much imagination," she said, "which
is a good thing really, considering the present I've bought
you."

"Is that for me?" I said, pointing to the parcel.

"You know it is. You've known it all along."

"I hoped . . . I've been trying hard not to look at it.
What is it?"

She came over to my bed and gave it to me.

"Open it and see. I had to buy it. I couldn't resist it."

I opened the parcel. Clare's present (I should have
guessed) was basically stationery. All bound up in stiff
covers with a marbled pattern on them like different colors
of melted ice cream: vanilla, chocolate, strawberry, and

pistachio. Nevertheless what it boiled down to was paper.
I said:

"It's really beautiful, Clare . . . but look, they've left out
the words. There's nothing in here. Could the story have
fallen out into the paper by accident?" I shook the wrapping around. "Come on out, you slippery little words . . .
what's happened to you?"

Clare laughed. "You're crazy. It's up to you to put the
words in. Or the pictures. Whichever you like."

"This is much too grand for me. You've never seen the
bits and pieces of paper I use. I don't think I've ever written
on anything other than the backs of other things, except
at school. I'd be shy, writing in a book like this."

"You'll get over it. Once you've covered the first page.
You'll see. It's only paper, after all."

(My sentiments entirely.)

"But what," I said, "am I supposed to write about? Very
little happens here on my island. I just lie about all day
under the palm trees and listen to the radio (my one luxury) and read the Bible and Shakespeare and my big
encyclopedia and look out there and see the wildlife passing by . . ."

"Exactly," Clare said. "You're bored. Invent something.
Write a story. Write poems. Write a diary. Keep a nature
notebook. It doesn't matter."

"Right," I said, "I will. And thanks, Clare. I know it's
only paper, but it *is* pretty."

Clare said: "I've got to go now. Mrs. Sandler will wonder what's become of me."

She left. Mrs. Sandler is her landlady, but she's worse
than any mother, the way she fusses over Clare. Mrs. Sandler's house looks like the cottage Hansel and Gretel found
in the wood. There are shutters on the windows with little

3

heart-shaped pieces cut out of them and the garden is full of trees: japonica, magnolia, almond, even a gigantic pine and a castor-oil tree. When you sit in the lounge, you could swear the whole place was underwater—full fathom five. The light that penetrates is green and dim and comes to you from far away. Clare has a room right at the top of the house. I went there once or twice during the summer. An ocean of greenery lay under her window then. Now, I expect it will change as autumn comes and some of the leaves begin to fall.

Thinking about Clare and her room reminds me of everything that's happened in the last couple of months. It's true that in this room, trapped on my island by a broken ankle, I often have the feeling that everything of any significance is happening somewhere else and to other people. When I get really low, I begin to think that nothing interesting has ever happened to me, but this is nonsense. I don't even really think it. Maybe what gets me down is this: the things that have happened to me have happened already, and what if nothing remotely like that ever happens to me again? Remotely like what? Like this past summer, that's what. Like being in *Three Sisters*.

The day before I broke my ankle was the day the set was struck and I went to look. I leaned against a wall and watched as the men took the flats out of the huge doors at the back of the theater, like so much old rubbish. I thought: they'll probably stash them away in a warehouse somewhere in case another play comes up which calls for nineteenth-century Russian-type scenery. There they were, those men, bundling up bits and pieces of the Prozorovs' house and garden (even the avenue of firs which I had helped to paint) into the back of a truck and tossing in a couple of boxes filled with props: the silver samovar,

4

lamps, rugs, cushions, even the screen from Act Three. Everything belonging to the three sisters had gone before you could say "Anton Chekhov." It was just as if the whole production had never taken place. I found the spectacle so depressing that I might even have cried, except that good old George kept popping out from his den at the Stage Door to see what was going on, and he nodded and smiled at me from time to time, so I stiffened my upper lip and convinced myself that what I was seeing wasn't sad in the least, simply a fact of theatrical life. And theatrical life was not in any way to be confused with "real" life.

In the theater, for a little while at least, you could travel. Anywhere. Into this time and that place, into the silken-scented courts of eastern princes, into stinking prisons, ships, schools, courtrooms, houses (grand and humble), into space, into prehistory—anywhere. And not only could you travel, you could also do what a great many people seemed to want to do most dreadfully: you could shed the person you were like a dress ("just hang it up behind the door as you go in, dear"—that was what Ruby used to say about the costumes) and step into someone more comfortable. Or more exciting. Or beautiful. Or wicked. Whatever. People would keep talking about the magic of the theater, and that day, watching the set disintegrate into bits of painted plywood and canvas in the back of a truck, I understood a little of what they meant. It was magic because it was ephemeral. Every single production, from the humblest to the most magnificent, disappears in the end, sliding down into nothing like a house of cards. Even if you managed to film a performance, that was what you would have at the end: one filmed show only. In the theater, something of the magic is to do with the fact that every single performance is unique. For instance, Tuesday's show will be different from Wednesday's because the leading lady has a stomachache. During Wednesday's matinée, a door will fall off its hinges and injure the toe of the poor old man playing the grandfather . . . so on and so forth. Nothing in the theater can ever be repeated exactly.

The truck drove away taking with it the last shreds of *Three Sisters*. I thought: no one will ever see it again the way we did it. Then I thought: never mind, the play is still there, the words are there, for other people to act out in their own way. A couple of rugs and an Ottoman thrown into some corner and forgotten have no significance at all.

The next day, like a bloody fool, I decided to pretend I was a tightrope walker, didn't I? And used the newly built wall outside the theater to practice on. The rest, as they say, is history.

Now the waves crash and roar and break all round my little lounge-island. Life is ebbing and flowing like a sea and stopping at my door. But I've started. See? Clare was right. I've written all these lovely little black words—flung out a net and brought in all this and put it down. I could do it again. I could get it down, bit by bit. Fish about. Arrange thoughts and feelings. Describe. Imagine. Make judgments. Stick them all together on this paper, scrap-book-fashion: my memories and thoughts about the summer. In between the melted ice-cream covers. Tell it like it was. Like I think it was.

It began in the kitchen. Almost everything begins in the kitchen. My mother said:

"No, but seriously, Mel, are you listening?"

"I haven't much choice, have I?" I said. "Not when you start. No sooner do you open your mouth than I see them: the audience. You always sound, when you talk, as if you think there's a crowd of people just lined up over by the nearest wall, ready to applaud. It's only me, you know."

"You," said my mother, scraping zucchini into a pot of something or other, and peering at me through the steam, "are lucky."

And you, I thought to myself, look like the flipping Queen of the Gypsies—gold earrings, silk headscarf, the works. I said:

"Why?"

"Most mothers don't talk to their daughters at all. Did you know that? There's what's called a communication problem. It's the generation gap . . ."

"I should be so lucky . . ." I muttered.

". . . but I've always made a special point of it. Talking to you, I mean, and this . . . well, this is something . . . I call it providential. As far as I'm concerned, it couldn't have come at a better time."

"What couldn't?"

"There, you see. I knew you weren't really listening. So now, pay attention. Project Theater are holding auditions tomorrow for *Three Sisters*. They're putting on what they call 'a young people's production.' Rehearsals going on all through the summer holidays and the show opening for four performances the first week in September. Couldn't be more convenient, now, could it, not if they'd designed it for you specially. And I can tell you another thing. It'll be a great weight off my mind, thinking you're happily occupied in the theater all day while I'm at work."

"Mum, I'm sixteen. I'm quite capable of looking after myself, you know. And anyway, you don't know they'll want me, do you? I don't really need this theatrical holiday camp."

"You think you don't," my mother said, "but you do.

Otherwise, I know exactly what'll happen: sleeping till eleven, stereo on all day, and hours and hours of what you're so good at—inspired milling around, with or without company."

"Without," I said. "Everybody's away. Everybody I like."

"There you are then," said my mother, stirring more chopped-up thingummies into the pot. Bubble, bubble, toil and trouble. "All the more reason for you to get involved in this production. You'll meet new people, find something both useful and pleasant to do with your summer. And what nonsense you talk. Naturally they'll want you. Also, I refuse, absolutely, to feel guilty about not giving you a summer holiday. I'm a one-parent family with a dress shop to run . . ."

"I'm not asking for a summer holiday."

"Good."

"But I don't see why you're trying to dragoon me into the theater just because you go all nostalgic and Judy Garlandish thinking of the greasepaint and stuff."

"I thought you wanted your name in lights. I can just see it: Melusine Herbert."

"Mel, for Heaven's sake, Mum. No one could afford the electricity for a stupid bloody name like Melusine. And you'd need the front of the theater to be a mile wide, just to fit all the letters in. Honestly, my father and his brilliant ideas . . ."

"He was a romantic."

"He was crazy. I know it doesn't do to speak ill of the dead, even if you have never met them. Specially not your own flesh and blood, but it's my belief that he'd no idea at all. He'd clearly totally forgotten what kids are like."

"But I agreed with him. At the time. We both thought it a beautiful, flowerlike name."

"You were both probably high on pot, lying around in long skirts on the grass, swapping daffodils and dreaming about San Francisco or the Himalayas. The Sixties. You realize, don't you, the tremendous amount of harm they've done to my generation. We're all going gray keeping our parents under some kind of control. I've got my hands full with you, you know. Middle-aged hippie."

"Nevertheless," said my mother calmly (hadn't she even been listening?), "you will go, won't you? Just go and see. It wouldn't hurt just to go and see what kind of a set-up they've got there . . . and I don't care what you say, you've got talent."

"But I want to direct. If I've told you once, I've told you a thousand times. I don't just want to act. Any old fool who's not embarrassed by looking ridiculous can spout the words out. It's directing . . . that's where you can . . . I don't know . . . shape things."

My mother sighed.

"That just shows how much you know. Firstly, it's not true that any old fool can spout the words. You're only able to say that because you find it so easy. And acting's more than that, anyway. It's a hell of a lot more than dressing up and pretending, and you'd find that out if you ever did any properly. Secondly, you've got to start some-where. Probably at the very bottom, sweeping the stage or something. Nobody, but nobody is going to come up to you at the bus stop and say: 'My goodness, it's the won-derful Mel Herbert. You are clearly just the person we're looking for to direct *Hamlet* at the National . . .'"

"Oh, Mum, don't be so silly. I know all that. I know I've got to start small. But honestly, how can I go all on my own to some theater and just stand up there and say: 'I want a part in your play.'"

"How?" My mother smiled. "Just go, that's all. If you

9

really want to, that's what you'll do. If you really want to, you won't let anything in the world stop you."

"But I don't know the play. How can I read for a part in a play I know nothing about?"

"I know it. I'll tell you all about it. I've even got a copy somewhere you can look at. It's about these three young women. They're all longing to get to Moscow. They never do, of course."

"It sounds," I said, "a giggle a minute."

"Read it," said my mother. "Read it and then see what you think."

Hours later I put down my mother's copy of *Three Sisters* and sat up on my bed to look out of the window. I'm not really crying, I told myself, not really, as I wiped my eyes to clear them of the tears that seemed (how, I had no idea) to have sprung up there. I stared at the monkey-puzzle tree that was the glory of the small, square garden behind our house. It was an oddity, out of place among the staid rhododendrons and ladylike puffs of hydrangea, a foreign-looking tree, spiky and dark and strange: exotic. I thought of the three sisters, out of place too in that dull little north-ern town, far from the lights and society of the city, of Moscow. I felt for them. I understood their predicament perfectly. All my life, it seemed, had been a harking back to something lost, something wonderful I had once had, and to somewhere else.

This lost dream of a place was better than here, better than a little suburban house (three up, two down, red-painted front door and obedient flowers in little cut-out circles of flowerbed) in a straight suburban street lined with trees, but it was distant in my memory. I'd last seen it the summer before my grandmother died, which was twelve years ago. I was four. It's possible I've remembered it all

10

wrong: the long field at the back of the house, climbing all the way up the hill, the tall grasses heavy with mauve and yellow flowers, the stream running down the hill and past the house and sparkling and chattering and bickering down the valley just as Tennyson's poem called "The Brook" said it did. It pleased me then that a poem could be so strictly accurate, and I still feel a satisfaction I cannot quite explain at the rightness of it, the pleasant *truth* of all the words, although it had been somewhat of a disappointment to discover that "haunts of coot and hern" meant only "where the birds (coot and hern were species of bird, apparently) lived" and not, as I'd thought then, a place haunted by two mysterious spirits with funny names. The house beside the stream, under the hill, among the tall grasses, the house where you could hide in twenty different rooms and attics and cellars and cubbyholes and sheds, had been sold years ago. The only physical reminder was the dolls' house. I think my grandfather made it for my mother. Once upon a time, I used to play with it, in my grandmother's house, and when she died, it came to this house and I had it in my room for years. At first I liked it and kept it neat and clean, but gradually I became less interested and the rooms grew dusty and neglected, little dolls were lost, or removed from their comfortable home to participate in other games, and the furniture broke, or disappeared and in the end, the shell of the house was taken up to the attic. I didn't miss it at all at first, but in the last few months I've thought about it more and more often, and wondered whether I shouldn't ask my mother to bring it downstairs so that I can set about restoring it to what it used to be. Perhaps I could turn it into the Prozorovs' old house in Moscow, the one the three sisters are longing to go back to.

As for my grandmother's house, the one to which I

always return in my imaginings, my mother and I keep memories of it alive by talking about it, and by telling one another lies about how one day we will go and find it again. Are Olga, Masha, and Irina aware that they are dealing in comforting dreams? By the end of the play perhaps they know that Moscow is an impossibility, and indeed that it is only the fact that it *is* so unattainable that makes it desirable. Vershinin says: *"Nor will you notice Moscow once you are living in it. Happiness is not for us and never can be. All we can do is long for it."* He also tells the story of a man in prison, writing with delight about the birds he can see from the window of his cell. Once he is free, of course, he ceases to notice them . . . Vershinin had known the girls' mother, now long dead. That means he must be much older than Masha, or quite a bit older. Perhaps he was very young when he met the three little girls, their hair braided and ribboned, all of them clustering around their pretty mother on the chaise lounge, with their brave and handsome father leaning against the mantelpiece. They must have been smiling, all of them, living in Moscow and having such a wonderful life . . .

I imagine Vershinin looking like my father. I may not have known my father to speak to, but I most certainly know what he looked like. He must have been tremendously vain. There are photos of him in piles and bundles and envelopes and albums all over the house, plus the large portrait in a frame that Mum still keeps on her dressing table. It reassures me to see it there. Its disappearance would mean a serious man in my mother's life, and although stepfathers haven't had such terrible press as stepmothers, there are still a couple of dreadful ones around in books.

I do think, though, that my father might have passed on a little more of his good looks to his only child. Reproduced himself a bit. I had a dishy dad and a mother who can pass with a kick and a shove in a flattering light, and look at me. I am no beauty. I am not ugly. I am not homely. I wouldn't describe myself as striking, or cuddly, or cute, or attractive, or sexy. I would describe myself as: OK. That's all. Plain, in the sense of not ornate. Undecorated. Tallish, not fat, not thin, hair brown, eyes brown, nose brown, mouth brown . . . well, all right, not really, but they might just as well be. Start again. Nose—straight. Mouth—six and a half out of ten. Teeth—well, yes, good, even, white UTTERLY BORING teeth. Who can get het up over teeth? Darling, your teeth send me into paroxysms of ecstasy . . . just one glimpse of her ivory canines filled him with such powerful surges of desire . . . ugh! And then there's the name. Melusine. I have fought all my life to be plain Mel, and I've succeeded so well that only at times of painful self-examination do I actually remember the namby-pamby, prissy-missy name my parents saddled me with at birth. On my first day at secondary school, a couple of unfortunate boys started a chant of "Mel-u-sine! Mel-u-sine!" during the lunch break. They were unaware, poor creatures, of three facts:

1. I'm not scared of anyone.

2. I have a wide vocabulary of words both long and rude and a loud voice to shout them in.

3. I'm very handy with my pointy-toed shoes (kicking) and my book-laden schoolbag (flailing out).

I had aimed a kick at Boy One while leveling my satchel at Boy Two's head, shouting obscenities and imprecations at the top of my voice. When the quailing lads were what I considered to be sufficiently cowed, I faced them where they stood, draped shivering beside a radiator. Nobly I resisted the temptation to hold them up by the lapels of their blazers. I said only:

"You two little pieces of putrid excrement get this straight. My name is Mel. Call me anything else and you'll find yourselves wearing a necklace of your very own teeth!"

I have been Mel to everyone ever since. Tomorrow at the audition, I thought, I'll lie outright. It's perfectly easy.

"Name, please," they'd say.

"Mel Herbert."

"Mel . . . is that short for anything?"

"No . . . just Mel."

"Mel . . . how unusual!"

Smiles all round. Simplicity itself. I shall never be Melusine again if I can help it.

I decided to try for Olga. She's the plain one, the eldest, the teacher, the one who looks after . . . who tries, at least, to look after the others. I have a lot in common with her. It isn't so much that I look after my mother. It's more that I organize myself, my image, to be pleasing to her, because I regard it as my duty to make my mother, if not happy, then at least not miserable on my account. So, I join in everything at school (choir, debating society, drama club) and even enjoy most of the activities while I'm actually doing them. I have friends, of course, but no one before this summer to whom I revealed what I like to think of as my innermost thoughts, picturing them as a flock of iridescent dragonflies locked up in an old wooden treasure chest, ready to fly out and flood the air with the shimmering colors of their wings, if only the right person comes along.

Before this summer, I'd found a distance springing up between myself and some of those girls I used to think were closest to me over the matter of boys. Quite suddenly, the thought uppermost in many minds was how to ensnare the attentions and affections of John/Pete/Fred, and never mind if John/Pete/Fred are nothing but callow youths with their minds mostly fixed on Kung Fu and football. I had not yet

14

met a boy who made my heart beat faster, and had even sometimes secretly worried that I might be abnormal in some way. At other times, thinking of certain film stars or fictional heroes (Vershinin, for instance, in his lovely uniform), I knew beyond question that I was capable of great feelings of love and passion, if only someone, someone possible, came along. Partly I wanted this to happen for my mother's sake. She had never said anything, but I had the feeling she was being deliberately tactful so as not to hurt me. I visualized her applying Vitamin E skin cream in front of her triple mirror every night and saying to my father's portrait: "Oh, darling, where have I gone wrong? Why is Mel not sweeping young men off the doorstep in droves? Why is she still so immature? What have I done to deserve a daughter who spends every Saturday night with me, instead of living it up at discos?" And so on and so forth.

The question was: would the Project Theater audition flush them out of the undergrowth, these handsome and sensitive young men I dreamed of, or would Vershinin and Tusenbach and Solyony have to be played by gangling, spotty, bedraggled kids? My mind boggled and continued boggling as I turned my attention to the problem of what to wear.

When Clare gave me this book yesterday, I wondered why she hadn't written anything in the front of it. Something like "With best wishes, from Clare" would have done nicely. I was a little disappointed. I shouldn't have been. I've just opened the book upside down (because with the swirly ice-cream covers it's hard to tell the back from the front) and there's the inscription. Not just any old "best wishes," either. It's a quotation, and Clare has written it in her skinny, elegant, tiny script, right on the inside of the back cover, in the bottom right-hand corner, so that it is the very last thing in the entire book. It says:

"*There must be happy endings: must, must, must!*"
Bertolt Brecht: *The Good Woman of Szechwan*

Brecht, I know (because we had read the *Caucasian Chalk Circle* at school), was a German playwright and all-round good bloke, but I don't know whether I agree with him or not. Clare never used to believe in happy endings.

16

Was this a sign that she now did? Or was she laughing at me? I thought about happy endings for a bit this morning and decided that, of course, there are no real endings at all. Not in life. Things drift into one another, eddying, swirling like the unseen currents in the oceans of the world. We like chopping things up into convenient, bite-sized chunks of time—beginnings and ends of years/weeks/months/terms/love affairs/illnesses, etc. I like the "time-like-an-ever-rolling-stream" notion, myself. Written-down stories are another thing altogether, of course. The writer has decided both where we will begin the book and where it will end, and it ends (in most cases) on the very last page. There are books, however, which never end—books where you feel so much a part of the world the writer has made for you, so much a friend of the characters, that you are convinced that somewhere, somehow, that book and the lives it contains are still going on.

Pictures are the same. The painter decides where the frame goes—how do we know there aren't even lovelier trees, houses, flowers or whatever just outside the boundaries the artist has decreed? We don't. We simply have to trust the artist. As for the happiness of endings, I'm deeply suspicious of them. Fairytales that end "and they lived happily ever after" are, to my mind, lying. I bet Cinderella and the Ugly Sisters are at each other's throats within two months of the wedding, and I don't hold up too much hope of a harmonious future to the wally who marries that silly little princess who couldn't sleep for the pea under her mattress. It seems clear that he is not going to be able to put a foot right his whole married life . . . ho, hum!

On the morning of the auditions, it was raining as I left the house. I made a mistake about the bus times and arrived at the Project Theater nearly an hour early. It's a square, red-brick building set in a landscape where everything is constantly in the process of being either put up or pulled down—it's very hard to tell which. There are little hillocks of gnawed-at bricks spread over waste ground, plywood fences enclosing dug-over bits of earth decorated with pieces of metal piping, and the sound of pneumatic drills rises above the noise of traffic from the main road. There are also houses that look as though they have been cracked open like nuts. Old wallpaper hangs in streamers from thin walls. You can still see the different patterns in all the rooms. Someone must have chosen them carefully once, looking through the books, comparing, imagining what they would look like when hung, and would the old curtains be all right with them, and now they had turned into porridge-colored messes in the rain and it wouldn't be long before the last walls would be crushed to nothing. Building and unbuilding.

Project Theater sat in the midst of this mess, with its small parking lot beside it, waiting for better days. The front of the place was locked and barred, but I looked through at the foyer and was a bit disappointed at the airport-lounge sort of chairs and general air of functional modernness. My idea of a theater is childish, but there you go. I would like them all to be old, red and gold, plump, velvety places, hung with chandeliers and with garlands of gilded fruit and flowers (plus lots of cherubs, ribbons, etc., etc.) swinging between tall columns and flinging themselves in profusion from one box to another and all round the galleries. I favor cherry-colored plush seats, curtains to match, and valances groaning with gold tassels. Probably I'd like a pantomime to be going on at the same time. This was not going to be that kind of place at all, I could tell. Rain was falling even harder by this time, so I made my way round to the back and found the Stage Door, flanked on each side by a little group of shiny-looking, well-kept dustbins, with the name of the theater stenciled on them in white paint.

When I opened the Stage Door, I found George, the Stage-Door keeper. Naturally, I didn't know he was called George then, but we had an entertaining chat which went, as far as I remember, something like this:

George: "You for the audition then, eh?"

Me: "Yes, I'm a little early, I'm afraid . . ."

George: "You're a little early." (It was at this point that it occurred to me that George was either hard of hearing or used to ignoring what young people were saying.) "Still, I suppose you can wait in the auditorium. No one's here yet. Are you going to make a mess, though, that's what I'd like to know . . . (sigh) . . . What're your shoes like? Are you going to leave mud on the carpet?" (He peered at my shoes. They must have come up to scratch, because he continued—) "I wish I had a penny, I do really, for every bit of litter I've picked up in there." (Pointing down a linoleum-lined corridor—) "Potato-chip wrappers, cigarette ends, silver paper, Kleenex, oh aye, they're a messy lot here right enough, and shall I tell you for why? Right then, it's because they're not proper actors and actresses, that's why. Not their fault, of course. It's the modern way. This here, this doesn't even feel like a proper theater. Where I used to work before, it had a proper name. The Alhambra, it was called. That's what I call a proper name. A name with a bit of glamour. Project . . . sounds like a bleeding laboratory, that does. And I tell you, there was a time when actresses had a bit of mink to put around their shoulders and wore proper high-heeled shoes and real jewelry and had flowers delivered to the Stage Door, and young men waiting for them outside. Nowadays, you can't tell who the blokes are, half the time . . . hair every length under the sun and even the lads wearing half a scrapyard of metal dangling from their ears . . . I don't know . . . Well, come on now . . . I'll show you where the auditorium is."

Me: "Thank you." (Writing it down like this shows my part in this dialogue to have been minimal. I may be mis-remembering. Maybe I said nothing. Maybe George had a monologue.)

George (over his shoulder while walking down the dark corridor): "If you ask me, they're looking for trouble, doing *Three Sisters* with a whole lot of kids. Probably put it in modern dress. Set it in a barracks in the Falkland Islands or something. They will keep doing it. Last year, they had a Chicago-gangster *Hamlet*. I dunno. Asking for trouble. There you are then. You wait in here. They'll all be along in a minute. Just sit down and don't eat anything in here, please."

Me: "Thank you." (I'm sure I said it that time.)

George disappeared and I did as he said and sat down in the dimly lit auditorium as unobtrusively as I possibly could. I chose a seat (dark blue plush) near the wall and waited for everyone to arrive. In spite of how small it was, and in spite of the total absence of overweight cherubs and gilded flowers, I decided, sitting there, that an empty the-ater was an enchanted place. The stage was full of possi-bilities. At the moment it looked like nothing so much as an area of gray-curtained space, but soon it would be alive with people, voices, and bodies to fill it with words and actions. Later still, paint and plywood would transform it, bewitch it, deck it out in all the trappings of a real room in a real house.

"Hello, down there," said a voice from out of the dark-ness behind me. "You're a bit on the eager side, aren't you? Have you come to audition?"

"Yes . . . I'm sorry . . . my bus came a bit early. I can't see you. Where are you?"

"Up here in the lighting box. It's OK. I'm coming down. Hang on a mo."

A few seconds later, he was sitting beside me.

"I'm Chris Taverner. I'm directing *Three Sisters*. What's your name?"

"Mel Herbert."

He wrote it down without batting an eyelid. "Did George show you in here?" he asked.

"Yes, he did. I didn't know his name though."

"Funny old geezer. You should get him talking about the old days in the theater. When actresses were actresses. He just misses all those chorus girls in feathers and little else, if you ask me."

"He said doing *Three Sisters* with a whole lot of kids was asking for trouble."

Chris laughed. "They all say that. All the bigwigs here were dead against it, till I convinced them."

"How did you do that?"

"Well, first off, I pointed out the relevance of the play. People like that, theater managers and boards of directors, love a bit of relevance. I told them *Three Sisters* was about what young people everywhere were best at doing. That is, dreaming—filling their days with illusions, hopes, aspirations that mostly come to nothing . . . learning to live with disappointment, with second best, without your heart's desire. Chekhov's play is about living in the future or the past, about the impossibility of grasping present happiness . . . all frightfully relevant to young people today, don't you think so?"

"Oh, I do, I truly do," I said, and I did. "But what about being able to do it? Can teenagers act those parts?"

"I don't see why not. People are always doing extraordinarily good school productions and no one is in the least surprised. I myself was a devastating King Lear when I was

21

sixteen. There wasn't a dry eye in the house by the time I'd finished. No, the awful thing is . . ." Chris's voice faded away and he seemed to have forgotten what he was saying. I didn't know whether to cough, or say something, or just sit still and hope that he'd remember he was in the middle of a sentence. I was just about to sniff gently when he went on:

". . . the thing is, I've imagined it all so clearly. I feel I *know* Olga, Masha, and Irina and I'll recognize them the moment I see them, as if they were real people that I met once and haven't forgotten. The Prozorovs' house is as familiar to me as my own flat . . . but it won't be like that. However hard I work, however hard everyone works, I'll *never* get what's up here—" (he tapped his forehead) "—onto this stage. I've learned. Directing a play is like carrying water in cupped hands from one receptacle to another. You lose half of it on the way."

The profundity of this statement robbed me of speech for a moment. By the time I thought of something intelligent to say, other people were beginning to file into the theater. Chris said:

"Nice talking to you . . . Mel, is it? See you on stage, then, eh? Good luck."

I could, I think, have lost my heart to Chris Taverner completely at this point. He looked exactly as I like men to look: like poets doomed to an early death from consumption. That is, thin, pale, dark-haired and with violet circles under brooding eyes. There can be variations, of course. Colors of hair and eyes don't matter nearly as much as the general air of fragility and exhaustion coupled with feverish energy, which Chris had in abundance. As things turned out, it was lucky I restrained myself. I was helped in this restraint by my first sight of Clare Bradshaw, staggering under a pile of stage plans and costume designs. She had come in with the first wave of auditionees and had taken the seat next to Chris. Even sitting down, I could see she was graceful, neat, quiet, and pretty in a delicate way that you might overlook if you weren't being careful. Chris certainly wasn't overlooking it. He kept stroking the nape of her neck so tenderly that I found myself blushing as I watched them. That was that, as far as I was concerned. Chris and Clare seemed to be a couple. I put myself firmly out of the running, not being much given to unrequited love, and concentrated instead on the character of Olga, which I was about to bring to blossoming life in front of everyone.

After so many weeks, it's difficult to recall whether there was anyone among all the people who came to audition who should have been in the company and wasn't. When you know everybody's performance inside and out, it's impossible to visualize it being done any other way. I remember an endless procession of girls, all shapes, sizes, voices, and boys likewise, but apart from the way he cast me, I would have chosen the same people as Chris did, which at the time I took to be a subtle indication of my obvious promise in the field of directing.

At the end of the afternoon, with the floor of the auditorium looking like one of George's nightmares, Chris went up on stage and read the cast list. Unfairly, I thought, he read it in the way a teacher reads a list of exam marks, leaving the best till last:

"Anfisa—Ruth Saunders
Ferapont—Charlie Mitchell
Second Lieutenant Fedotik—Peter Barking
Second Lieutenant Rode—Derek Marshall
Dr. Chebutykin—Roland Sweet

Junior Captain Solyony—Johnny Gates
Lieutenant the Baron Tusenbach—Simon Bowes
Lieutenant Colonel Vershinin—Mike Corderly
Kulygin—Andrew Stanton
Andrey Prozorov—Matt Arlen
Natasha—Mel Herbert
Irina—Dinah McLaren
Masha—Louise Flynn
Olga—Tricia Dickinson."

For a second I didn't know whether I could keep myself from crying. I had wanted so much to be Olga, had pictured myself in the part so convincingly, had read it so movingly just an hour or so ago, that I felt wounded and hard done by, my talents unrecognized. These sentiments soon gave way to wild elation as I listened to Chris thanking all the unsuccessful auditionees for coming, and watched them all, droves of them it seemed to me, filing mournfully out into the rain. I was in. I was one of the Cast. I was Natasha, common, brassy, mercenary, grasping, and insensitive. Also badly dressed. And adulterous. Well, well. I braced myself mentally. Could I do Natasha? Would Chris help me? Panic filled me. I remember, just for an instant, wanting to rush home and never leave my house again, rather than disgrace myself on a public stage.

To distract myself, I looked around at those of us who were left: the Cast. I looked at Olga, Masha, and Irina and in particular at Olga and I had to admit a) that they looked just right and b) that they looked like sisters. All three were fair. Tricia Dickinson, who did look older than the other two, was placid—honey-colored and plump. Louise Flynn's hair was on that wonderful borderline where gold becomes red, and her face was thin and intense. Her gray eyes flashed and sparkled and her hands moved nervously

24

all the time. And Dinah? It's hard to write dispassionately about her now, but that day at the audition, I thought she was the loveliest person I had ever seen. She was tiny for a start, and graceful. Her eyes were like summer seas, winter skies, aquamarines, sapphires—any or all of those. Her skin was satin/velvet/peaches and cream and there was precisely the right distance between one eye and another, between nose and mouth, between mouth and chin—perfect proportions. Her gold/honey/corn-colored/sun-kissed curls positively lit the place up. She was wearing a flowered dress, pale tights, and white flat pumps. Most other people (girls too) were in variations on denim themes, which made Dinah stand out like a tulip growing in a prison yard. Later on, when I knew her better, I realized that this was an effect she had worked hard to create, sitting for hours in front of her mirror, planning the strategy of her appearance as carefully as any general laying plans for battle. Later . . . well, later everything was different, but that day I thought of Dinah as the embodiment of springtime, youth, and innocence. So much for my perceptions.

Chris called the first rehearsal for the next day at ten o'clock. Thanked us all very much. Looked forward to working with us. Told us to read the play through and have some ideas about it before morning. Smiled. And then we all left. At least, I think we did. I have a picture in my mind: a picture that I think I saw as I looked back into the auditorium from the double doors leading to the foyer. Perhaps my feelings and subsequent events have colored my memory. Perhaps I only dreamed it and have stitched it into my mind as a real fact—I don't know. I have a mental image of Chris leaning back against the stage and Dinah, swaying toward him like a reed, tilting up her head and talking to him. He's nodding and smiling down at her. She's so little that almost every man she meets has to smile down at her. Her small white hands are making patterns in the air. And then there's Clare. She's in the picture, too: sitting very straight in the middle of the front row. Waiting. Unrelaxed.

I left the theater and ran through the muddy wasteland to the main road to catch the bus home. After standing all on my own at the stop for about ten minutes, I began to doubt the existence of buses. I hadn't even seen one going in the opposite direction. I thought: I'll give it another five minutes and start walking, and then a battered blue Mini drew up at the curb and Clare leaned out of the window.

"Mel, isn't it? You'll get absolutely drenched if you stand there any longer . . . come on, I'll give you a lift home."

"Will you really? Terrific!" I said, and got in as quickly as I could. "I'm a bit wet already, actually. I hope it doesn't wreck the seat."

Clare snorted. "This old rattletrap? You're kidding. It's got no upholstery to speak of. I'm the one who generally apologizes to my passengers. I warn them that they wear their clothes in this car entirely at their own risk. Where do you live then?"

It turned out that we lived in neighboring streets. I'd never seen Clare before, but I knew the house at the corner of Ashfield Avenue.

"I stare at it each time I go past," I told Clare. "I just can't believe anyone really wants all those trees pressing round the house like that. It must be pitch-dark all the time."

"I don't think Mrs. Sandler, my landlady, believes in daylight," Clare said. "She has these beautiful antique lamps with pearly glass shades all over the place, and I think she likes to pretend she's living in the middle of a forest. Perhaps she's really a witch and all those wonderful meals she gives me are simply fattening me up for when

26

she wants to roast me. Come and meet her, if you've got time."

I went. I couldn't resist it. Mrs. Sandler was not a witch, of course, but from that day onward I thought of the house as Hansel and Gretel's cottage. It wasn't precisely made of gingerbread and sugared almonds, but Mrs. Sandler was like an absurd overstatement of a mother, who not only fussed, cajoled, scolded, and loved ten times more than any mother I'd ever seen, but also baked cinnamon plaits, crumbly biscuits, and sponges so light that it was only the weight of the icing on them that anchored them to the plate. We'd hardly crossed the threshold into the crepuscular hall that day, when she appeared and whisked us both into the lounge "to have a little something."

Clare managed to get us out of there in twenty minutes, during which time I had admired everything: the black carved furniture, photographs of relatives in stiff hairstyles, and a cupboard full of china dolls' house furniture decorated with gold squiggles and tiny pink flowers.

When we reached Clare's room at the top of the house, I stood inside the door for a moment, just staring.

"Come in," said Clare. "I'm sorry it's such a mess."

"I don't think it's a mess. I think it's marvelous. I spend hours and hours trying to get my room to look like this. There's so much in it." I shook my head in disbelief at all the treasures.

Clare laughed. "Most people would call it a mess."

"Then they're crazy," I said. Clare's room looked as though someone had tipped cardboard boxes full of silk shawls, peacock feathers, rings, dried flowers, necklaces, pebbles, swatches of velvet, lace, brocade, silk, chiffon, cut-glass perfume bottles, patchwork cushions, Chinese vases, knitted afghans, and thick paper in twenty different colors into a small space, and given the whole thing a thorough stir with a giant spoon. In the middle of the floor was what appeared to be a box with a piece of material thrown over it.

'Whatever's that?" I asked.

"A model of the set," Clare said, "but I can't show you, I'm afraid. It's still got a bit of work to be done on it. I'll find the sketches for the costumes, though . . . you can have a look at them if you like."

"Yes, please."

"And let's have a drink, shall we? If you're not too full of cake. I think these glasses are OK."

I sat down carefully on a cushion and tried to drink my sherry nonchalantly, as though drinking sherry in the afternoon was something I did every day as a matter of course.

"Clare," I said (perhaps made bold by the couple of teaspoons of alcohol I'd managed to sip), "will you tell me how old you are?"

"I'm twenty-three," she said.

"Really? You look much younger than that," I said and immediately regretted it. What if she'd been striving to look thirty?

"Well, I feel about a hundred and twenty. It's this show. I always get like that when I'm involved. It's nice of you to say that, though . . . I suppose it's being small. I think people automatically think smallness goes with youth, don't they?"

I nodded. "Have you worked for Project for a long time?"

"About two years. I came up here from London when my marriage broke up. I think I had the idea that the farther away I went physically, the easier it would be to get over . . . all that."

For a moment, I couldn't think of anything to say. Marriage? Broken up? Getting over? Then I said (and probably it was the unaccustomed booze that had loosened my tongue), "I'm sorry . . . I didn't realize. I'd thought maybe we could be friends."

Clare chortled. "I've heard of a stigma being attached to divorce, but this is ridiculous. Why on earth shouldn't we be friends?"

"Well, you're . . . that is, you've been . . . and I'm only . . . you know . . . young and so on. What I mean is, wouldn't you feel it's beneath your dignity to be friends with a mere teenager?"

"You are a hoot, honestly, Mel," Clare said. "It isn't age that makes differences between people. Perhaps you *are* young after all . . ."

"No, I'm not. I'm getting older every day."

"That's true. You'll see, anyway, while we're doing the play: all that kind of differences, differences that mean a lot to people outside the theater, simply evaporate. Age, race, class . . . they're not important. I mean, I'm not saying there won't be people you can't stand. There will be. But those sorts of things, the unimportant things, fall away in the theater because you're working at something together and it becomes more important than anyone's feelings. No, in the theater, if you can't stand a person, it's generally for a very good reason. Like they're bloody awful."

I nodded wisely. I wanted to get back to the subject of her marriage. Why had it broken up? And what about Chris? I said: "I think Chris is lovely. Are you going out with him? Do you mind me asking?"

Clare was standing at the desk with her back to me. She said nothing for such a long time that I thought I'd gone too far and said more than I should have done. I was wondering sadly if she'd still want to be my friend when she answered in such a soft voice that I had to lean forward to hear her.

"I don't mind you asking. Chris and I . . . well, we are going out together in a way."

"In a way?"

"It's complicated. I suppose I'm nervous. I'm only just getting over Phil . . . my ex-husband . . . and I think I'm reluctant to commit myself. I don't know. I don't want to be hurt again. I don't want to risk it." She laughed. "It's a bit silly really. I don't imagine there's such a thing as loving someone without being hurt. I don't suppose I ought to be putting you off like this as you're so young. Don't pay any attention. It's only me being cynical. Love is really quite as nice as they say it is in all the songs, only you are extremely vulnerable. It's as if you're much thinner-skinned than usual."

"I can hardly wait. It sounds a proper treat."

Clare smiled. "No, I'm very fond of Chris and, well, he's working on me. I don't know what will happen. I don't truly know what I want."

"D'you know what I think?" I said. "I think that bit of the play where Irina tells Tusenbach she'll marry him, but she doesn't really love him, I think it's one of the saddest bits of all."

"Yes, poor Baron! Irina's heart is like a grand piano, all locked up, she says, and the key's lost, and he says the lost key gives him sleepless nights . . . Do you think he's happier dead? Better off?"

"No, of course not. I'm an optimist. I think if he'd lived, he'd have married Irina and she'd have fallen in love with him in the end . . ."

"You *are* young, aren't you?" Clare said. "You still believe in happy endings."

"Only in stories," I said, trying to sound as grown-up as I could. "Not necessarily in real life."

"Don't get cross. It's not a crime to be an optimist. And it's true that *Three Sisters* is only a play, but I've thought and thought about them all such a lot, they seem almost real to me. I dream about them sometimes. I even dream about their old house in Moscow and their mother . . . I can see them, those sisters, when they were little girls. I think Vershinin was in love with their mother when he was a young soldier . . . and he falls in love with Masha because she reminds him of the mother. The Doctor was in love with her long ago when they were all young . . . he says so in the play. Oh, I'm just rattling on. I get carried away. I'm sorry. I'll find you those sketches of the costumes and then you can see what you'll be wearing. Hang on a second."

She began to look through papers on her desk. The sun had decided, now it was late afternoon, to come out for a quick half hour or so before nightfall and was shining through the window onto Clare's unmade bed. I was struck by the picture it made: lacy curtains held in two curves, like falls of hair drawn back, and the sheet set into dips and peaks and swirls like white frosting on a cake, with dark shadows on the far side of the pillows.

"Here you go," Clare said at last, and gave me a dozen sheets of bond paper. I stared and stared at the delicate lines and washes of color and at the edges of the pages where Clare had drawn in details: Natasha's dreadful green belt, Vershinin's military medals, the Doctor's tatty old velvet jacket. She had also stuck down scraps of cloth: a piece of lace from Irina's Act One dress, a fragment of navy blue from Olga's skirt.

"They're fantastic," I said. "Will I really look like that?"

"It's never exactly the same as the picture you have in

your mind. A fair approximation, that's the best you can hope for."

"Chris said almost the same thing today. About getting his idea of the play onto the stage."

"Well, naturally we've talked about it and argued about it endlessly—the play, I mean—and that is something we agree about."

I didn't want the afternoon to end, but I had to go home at last.

"Ask me for a lift whenever you like," Clare said. "Come and see me whenever you like." She took me downstairs and saw me to the front door.

"Just in case," she whispered, "Mrs. Sandler is lurking in the kitchen with a plate of cream horns, ready to attack."

" 'Bye," I said. "And thanks so much. I really think your room is lovely. And your designs."

I walked home wishing I could have told Clare what I really felt: that being in her room had made me feel as if the inner corners of my life had been touched with gold paint and were glittering away silently where no one else could see them.

"I haven't even thought about supper," said my mother as I let myself in at the back door. "I've been so on edge . . . you're ever so late . . . did the auditions really go on till now?"

I started to say, "No, but . . ." and tried to explain about the buses and Clare, but she wasn't having any of that.

"Tell me all excuses later, please. Now I'm only interested in one thing—are you in?"

"Did I get a part, do you mean?"

My mother growled. "Why are you doing this to me? Don't you realize the suspense I've been in? I've been like this all day. Probably I'll go into the shop tomorrow and find I've sold the stock at half price. People could have cheated me today left, right, and center, did they but know it."

"Well, if you'll keep quiet for a couple of minutes—yes, I know it's hard, but do try—if you'll just be patient, I'll tell you the news."

She covered her mouth with her hands, as if to stop the words coming out in spite of her, and nodded eagerly.

"OK," I said, "you can relax. I'm in. Natasha. I wanted Olga. That's what I read for, but I'm pleased to be in, anyway." I'd heard of people jumping for joy, but I'd never seen it happen till that moment. She sprang from her chair and began to bounce all over the kitchen. I said:

"Mum, honestly, stop it. What if someone saw you through the window? Whatever would they think? A woman of your age!"

"I don't care," she sang out. "I'm happy, and I don't care who knows it."

Sometimes I have to keep my mother's ebullience under control. This was clearly such a time. I used the most tempting bribe I could think of.

"Sit down," I said, "get yourself a cup of tea or something and sit down, and then I'll tell you every detail about everyone."

"Yes, yes," she said.

"But you're not to say a word until the end. OK? No interrupting at all. Right?"

"Promise."

We sat down and I told her everything. I enjoyed it. My mother has her faults, but she's a marvelous audience. She nods, smiles, laughs, looks worried, cries, and groans at all the right places. By the time I'd finished, I was exhausted, both from talking so much, and from having to watch the reactions my story produced.

"Well," she said, "it all sounds terrific, and I must say, I like the sound of Clare. I think you should invite her for supper one night, if she's all alone in a studio apartment, not eating properly."

"You obviously weren't listening when I told you about Mrs. Sandler's cooking."

"I was . . . only I didn't mean just food, silly. I meant company. It can't be much fun for her, can it, just her and her landlady every night. Sounds a bit claustrophobic to me."

"I don't know if she'll want to come though. I hardly know her. I'll feel strange asking her."

"Don't be such a ninny. From what you say, she's very easy to talk to . . . very friendly. Ask her round for Sunday night, the very next time you see her. What's the worst that can happen?"

I said: "She won't be able to come."

"Exactly. Not a disaster. So ask her. Right?"

"Right," I said.

I thought Clare probably would accept. I hoped she would. I'd only just met her, but already I felt closer to her than to many of my old friends. She was the kind of person with whom it's hard to be anything but your real self. There was no pretending necessary with Clare. I knew that, even from my short time with her.

The next day at ten (or thereabouts—why are so many people incapable of getting anywhere on time?) we assembled for a reading of the play. The rehearsal room was large and white with a wooden floor and nothing in it except a whole lot of canvas chairs and some ashtrays. I was one of the first to arrive, so I chose a chair in the corner and waited to see what would happen next, worrying a little that the whole thing was a dreadful mistake, and that Chris would look at me and say: "Natasha? In this production? You must be joking!" I pushed these silly fantasies away firmly. If I had indulged them at all, I would have been out of the theater quicker than you could say "Moscow." As we gathered, I was reminded strongly of the very first day at a new school. No one knew anyone, no one spoke to anyone else, people were careful not to let their eyes meet, some seemed fairly embarrassed, and some looked panic-stricken.

Louise and Andrew arrived together. They were holding hands and talking. I deduced from this that a) they knew each other and b) they liked each other. Dinah came and sat next to me, even though there were lots of other chairs free. She smiled charmingly at me straight away. I felt immensely proud and flattered. I'm not going to be The Girl Most Likely, I thought, but it certainly is the next best thing to be her best friend. I smiled charmingly back at Dinah and decided, what the hell, I may as well speak. I said:

"Isn't it like the first day of term?"

Dinah giggled. "It is a bit, I suppose. But we never had a teacher who looked like Chris . . . are you still at school?"

I hated to admit it, but I had to. Dinah said: "I left last year. I'm absolutely thrilled about this part, because I'm determined to be a film and TV actress, and my mum and dad think it's all just talk and they want me to help behind the counter in the shop. If I hadn't got this part . . ." Dinah shuddered, ". . . well, anyway, they were quite pleased, really. Perhaps they'll see I'm serious now."

"What kind of a shop?"

"It's a sweetshop."

"How fantastic!"

"Everybody says that, but it's not. You get sick of the sight of chocolate, and that's a fact." She looked around, then turned to me again.

"What do you think of this play, then?"

"I think it's very . . ." I thought a bit to see if I could come up with the right word. I couldn't. I said, "sad," in the end because it was the closest.

"Well, yes." Dinah agreed. "I suppose it is in a way, but you do feel sometimes, don't you, that those three need a kick up the backside. I mean, there they are, dying to go to Moscow . . . I feel like saying: why don't you go then? Eh? Get on a train and go if that's how you feel."

"But that's the whole point of the play," I said as calmly as I could. Dinah hadn't understood at all. "They *can't* go. The play's about all the different reasons that they can't: because of work and money and relationships and . . ." Chris fortunately came in at this point with a short, dark-haired young woman carrying a clipboard, and I stopped talking. Perhaps he would explain it to Dinah. He was the director. It was his job.

"Right, everybody," Chris said and smiled in our general direction. Because of Dinah? "This is it. It doesn't look like much, does it? I don't know whether any of you have done any work in the theater before, and it doesn't really matter, but I'll tell you a few things which may surprise you. First of all, I'd like to introduce Janet Blake, who is the Stage Manager on this show and we're lucky to have her. She's the one (in case some of you don't know what a Stage Manager does) who makes sure that everything happens on the stage in the proper order: lights go on and off, actors go on and off, curtains open and close. In short, the lot. She manages the stage." Janet smiled modestly and looked down at her clipboard. Chris went on:

"Now, the first thing I want to reassure you about is this: all of you will be as easy with one another, as uninhibited as members of a family within the next couple of days. You'll see so much of one another that you'll begin to feel as though the rest of the world has never existed and does not exist. I'm not saying you'll love each other. Of course you won't, but you certainly will know each other. The second thing is that contrary to popular opinion, working on a play is bloody hard work and anyone who's not prepared for it had better leave now. And it's not only hard, it's thankless and boring, too. Sixty percent of your time will be spent hanging around: waiting for your scene to be done, waiting for your costume to be fitted, waiting, waiting, waiting. Then the other forty percent, when you're not hanging around, you'll be rehearsing, and then you'll wish you *were* still hanging around, because I'm going to take you through those words so many times and in so many ways you'll think you've taken up residence in a humming top. We open six weeks from tonight. I want no copies of the play on stage after the first three weeks of rehearsals. OK?" Chris smiled. "That, you see, takes care of the little spare time you *do* have—you'll be learning your parts, won't you?" Everyone laughed. "Good. Let's get started. It's a May morning. The sun is shining. It's Irina's name day. What could be better? Begin, please . . ."

Tricia Dickinson spoke Olga's first words almost in a whisper, but the play had begun:

"It's exactly a year since Father died . . ."

By the time she had spoken the last words, it was all I could do to keep from crying. During the bit where Masha and Vershinin say good-bye to one another, I looked at Dinah and her lips were trembling, too.

"That was good," said Chris. "It'll be much better than that of course, but it's good. Has anybody got anything to say? Or to ask? OK then, I'll give you all the rehearsal schedule for the next week and we'll discuss the play and what it's all about in more detail tomorrow."

Dinah turned to me. "Can you come round to my house this afternoon, do you think? You seem to know a lot about this play. Can I pick your brains, would you mind?"

"No, I'd love to," I said. I was quite disappointed that the read-through was finished and that was it for the rest of the day.

"About three o'clock, then. Here's the address." She picked up my clipboard (Yes, I had one, too. I'd come equipped to make notes . . . oh, it was exactly like school, and I was the most eager First Former) and wrote her address on the top sheet of paper.

"Great," I said. "See you then."

Dinah glided over to where Chris was sitting talking to Tricia and Roland Sweet. I felt let down. What was I supposed to do for the next couple of hours till it was time to go to Dinah's? There was no one at home and not much in the fridge as far as I remembered.

"Hello, I'm Mike," said someone and I looked up and there was Vershinin. I'd been quite surprised at how good he'd been in the read-through, because he didn't strike me as immediately irresistible. But he had a nice smile. Perhaps he would grow on me.

"Hello."

"Would you like to come and have a sandwich or something? Louise and Andrew are going round to the Capricorn, which is that café round the corner."

"Yes, I'd love to," I said, thinking that if we were going to get to know each other that well, we'd better make a start. As we left the theater, Dinah was deep in conversation with Chris and Tricia and Roland. I heard Louise say to Andrew: "Guess who's going to be Teacher's Pet, then?" Andrew laughed.

Louise couldn't stay long.

"She's always got to babysit for that brat of a little niece of hers," said Andrew. "She's the youngest, you see. There's Noreen, who's the eldest, and she's got two little boys, and then Christine, that's the brat's mother."

"Is she at work, then?" I asked. "Christine?"

"Well," said Andrew, "she is, but it doesn't make much

difference really. Even when she's not at work, she's too busy looking after her appearance to worry about little Lorraine."

"What about Louise's mother?" I asked.

"She works, too," Mike said.

"At a pub called the Yellow Parrot," Andrew added. "Her dad ran off years ago."

I said: "Do you all go to the same school? You seem to know each other so well."

"Yeah," said Mike, "but I'm in the next class up. Andrew and Louise are in the same class. Andrew fell in love with Louise when he was five years old."

Andrew blushed but didn't deny it.

"He'd never seen," Mike continued, "such a pretty little girl before—he's only got brothers. Anyway, one look at those red curls was too much for him and at milktime he stroked her cheeks and lost his heart forever."

"Geroff," said Andrew, smiling.

"Well, it's true," said Mike, "and it's also true that it's thanks to Andrew that we came to the audition."

"Right," said Andrew. "I was the one who saw the notice just flapping about on the board outside the Hall at school. I persuaded them to come because I wanted to be in it so much . . ." A huge grin spread over his features. "Hey, we're all in it . . . I've just realized. Isn't that great?"

"Andrew," said Mike, "has been stagestruck ever since he and Louise appeared together in a Nativity Play about ten years ago. He really liked all that dressing up, and learning songs, and slapping greasy stuff all over his face and everything, so he joined the Drama Club at school, in spite of all kinds of stupid remarks people kept making about it being only for posers or pansies or stiffs or snobs."

"Do you go?" I asked Mike.

"Yeah, sure."

"Don't people make remarks about you?"

"They used to."

"What happened?"

"I thumped a couple of them and they shut up after that."

I looked at him for other signs of Clint Eastwoodery, but he seemed perfectly ordinary to me: tall, slim, freckled . . . nothing to get excited about. But good, dark brown eyes that looked straight at you and a smile that was rare enough to seem like a compliment or a gift when it did appear. I said:

"Do you all live near one another?"

"Louise and I live on the Green Lane estate," said Andrew. "Louise lives on the sixth floor of her block of flats, and I live on the fourth floor of another block just across from it. We can wave at one another from our kitchen windows."

That reminded me of Gerda and Kay in the story about the Snow Queen and how their houses had been so near to one another that rose trees had grown between the attic of one house and that of its neighbor, and the children had sat on little stools in the shadow of the rose trees and played together, loving one another more than brother and sister. I knew Green Lane. Huge gray tower blocks, and concrete paths between them. The road bridge over the motorway passes right near Green Lane. At night you can see a chain of headlights unrolling toward the horizon, and the orange streetlamps shine on shards of glittery broken glass. No bridges of roses there between one house and another. *No sirree.*

Dinah's street was lined with featureless, nondescript shops: hardware stores, greengrocers, launderettes, and corner shops masquerading as supermarkets with piles of

41

wire baskets inside the front door. From the outside, McLaren's Confectionery looked quite unremarkable, but because of Dinah's parents, I think of the shop as being something out of a book by Beatrix Potter. I called them Daddy Mouse and Mummy Mouse to myself the second I met them, standing with bright eyes behind the counter, with the pear drops and the cola cubes and the pastel colors of the sugared almonds and craggy brown rocks of peanut brittle towering around them.

"Mel, isn't it?" said Daddy Mouse, stretching out a plump paw. He was altogether a sleek, small, chubby little creature, with a gray moustache (*mouse*tache!) and pink cheeks and a striped gray and black waistcoat pulled tight over his stomach. "Our Dinah's in the back. Enid'll show you, won't you, dear? Go on, I can manage without you now. I'll be in for tea shortly. You go on now."

Mummy Mouse scuttled out from behind the counter. She wore an oatmeal-colored skirt and a gray hand-knitted cardigan. She was small and thin, like Dinah, and behind the pebble glasses she wore, her eyes were blue. Faded, yes, but unmistakably blue. I wondered whether, in about a hundred years, Dinah would look like that: like an anxious and kindly little rodent. It was hard to believe.

"I'll just go and tell Dinah you're here, dear. Do sit down," she said. "I think she's just finished doing her hair."

"Thank you."

"It's grand though, isn't it, about the play," she said suddenly and all in a rush, blushing as though she'd been steeling herself to say something for ages and had at last dared to do it. "I'm that pleased for our Dinah. We're ever so proud. I can hardly wait to see her in it. She says they don't know what they're wearing yet. I asked her."

"Irina—that's who Dinah is—" I volunteered, "starts

by wearing white . . . right at the beginning. It's her name day. Like a Russian birthday."

"White . . ." The mouse-face lit up into a smile. "How lovely! Our Dinah'll look smashing in white." She shook her head. "I don't know why I'm going on like this, love. Only I'm that proud. I'll go and get Dinah. Just you sit down here for a moment or two."

The walls of the lounge were hung with needlepoint pictures: swans on a lake, a castle, a galleon under full sail, a vase with flowers in it. I didn't know for certain, but I could just imagine Mrs. McLaren sitting here in the evenings, not watching the television, stabbing the printed canvas with a silver needle in her dainty little paws. She came back into the lounge after a few moments and said:

"Dinah says you can go up, dear. It's just on the right at the top of the stairs."

They say, don't they, that you can tell a person's character from their room: what they have in it, how it's decorated and so on. I know that I often put stuff here and there in order to impress people. Once, I put a chessboard in the corner with a difficult problem set out on it, taken from the newspaper. This was done specifically to dazzle a boy called Mark, but obviously the problem was too complicated or something. He took one look at it and (metaphorically speaking) you couldn't see him for dust. He certainly never came to visit me again.

On Dinah's room, you could see, her mother had lavished all the love she felt, as well as most of the money the family possessed. Dinah had a dressing table with a lacy, flounced skirt-thing around it, white lacy curtains, wallpaper printed with roses, and a soft, fluffy pink carpet. Dinah's necklaces hung over a corner of her mirror and she had a white china hand to put her rings on. I thought it looked faintly sinister, chopped off at the wrist like that, but it was definitely intended to be pretty. Dinah's clothes lived in a white cupboard. If I'd been Mummy Mouse, I would have wept every time I came in, though. Dinah, totally unimpressed with her mother's idea of decor, had covered every available bit of wall and cupboard door with cuttings from the kind of magazine that has glossy pages and clothes that most people would have to take out a mortgage to buy. Not only were there herds of whippet-thin women with unnaturally shiny skins and sticky, sulky mouths, there were also color photographs of jewels, shoes, the fronts of various mansions, gardens with undulating lawns, and even pictures of food: stews set about with jewel-colored vegetables, wine in crystal glasses . . . I couldn't take my eyes off the display.

"Everybody stares like that at first," Dinah said.

"Well, it's something to stare at," I answered. "It must have taken you ages, all that cutting and sticking."

"I like it . . . I like pretending it's me—dressing like that, living like that." She smiled. "Don't you ever pretend things?"

"Yes, of course," I began weakly.

Dinah looked serious and said: "I'll tell you what I sometimes think, shall I? Only please don't tell anyone. I've never told a soul before." She looked around as if to search out hidden spies.

"I won't say a word," I promised.

"Well, I sometimes think that I've been adopted. That my parents are not my real parents. That they adopted me when I was tiny because my real mother couldn't look after me."

"Then who," I managed to say, "is your real mother?"

"I've thought and thought about that. In the end I de-cided that it must have been a really beautiful and suc-

44

cessful actress who didn't want to ruin her career by having an illegitimate baby . . ." Dinah's voice faded away. Then she laughed. "Don't look so shocked, silly. I *know* it's not really true. I just like to imagine sometimes, that's all. I had you worried for a second there, didn't I? But I can see that I look like my mother a bit. Can you see it at all?"

I could, of course, but I'm not thick.

"I don't see any resemblance whatsoever," I said firmly and Dinah was satisfied.

After tea, Dinah and I discussed the play: everybody's character and why the sisters could never get to Moscow. During the afternoon there were two small conversations which struck me as important at the time and which have come back to me now. The first happened during tea. Daddy Mouse had been talking about "that Commie play" even though I'd explained to him as carefully as I could (and without losing my temper as I generally do when I hear an ill-considered and blanket condemnation of everything like "Commie") that *Three Sisters* was written fifteen years before the Russian Revolution. Then out of the blue, Mummy Mouse turned to me and said:

"I don't suppose they'd need any help, would they, up at the theater, with sewing the costumes and all? I'm handy with a needle, even if I say so myself. Do you think I should go and ask up there . . . ooh, I'd love to see what it's like, behind the scenes and everything. You wouldn't like to ask them for me, would you, Dinah dear?"

Dinah paused with a spoonful of tinned pineapple halfway to her mouth. I'll never forget the look that crossed her face. I'd heard of "aghast" in books, but had never seen it before. It was worse than "worried" or "disgusted" or "shocked." Dinah was aghast. It's just the right word. It even sounds right. Ghastly. Aghast. She said only:

"It's a professional theater, Mum. They've got wardrobe

people and all that to do stuff like costumes. They won't need any outside help."

"Crushed" is how Dinah's poor mother looked. Another good word. Smaller. Flattened. As though Dinah had squashed something inside her. I couldn't even finish my pineapple rings, I felt so depressed.

The second conversation took place at the bus stop. Dinah had come to see me off.

"What do you think of Clare?" she asked. "Do you think she's pretty?"

I was still angry with Dinah for her unkindness to her mother. I knew exactly what she wanted me to say, so I said the opposite. "Yes, she's lovely," I smiled. "Don't you think she is? Chris certainly does. I went around to her place yesterday and she told me all about it. She and Chris are going out together." Dinah smiled enigmatically in a way which meant: I know something you don't know. Then the bus came.

When I got home, I toyed with the idea of getting the dolls' house down from the attic and turning it into a replica of McLaren's Confectionery. Perhaps, I thought, I shouldn't blame Dinah for pasting her walls with images from the lives of the disgustingly rich. I, too, would have suffered a kind of claustrophobia in that place: like Alice in Wonderland, I'd have felt like growing and growing and pushing my hand through the walls as if they were paper, and watching the Marley floor tiles and the ever-so-bright-and-cheerful curtains with a pattern of smiley-faced pots and pans come crashing down around my head.

As I fell asleep that night, Mike Corderly's smile came into my mind. He had, I realized, told me nothing at all about himself. He had not even answered my question and told me where he lived.

On Sunday night, Clare came to our house for supper. I'd plucked up courage and telephoned her at Mrs. Sandler's house the morning after I'd been to Dinah's.

All of Sunday, I hung around my mother in the kitchen, making sure she was cooking things that were delicious without being too showy. I didn't want Clare to think she'd come to a formal dinner party, but on the other hand, I did want special food for her.

"Please," I said to my mother, "homemade chocolate mousse."

"Made it last night," she said, "so there."

"Go to the top of the class, then," I answered.

"And my scrumptious beef casserole."

"It's lucky Clare's thin," I said. "Do you need any help?"

"You could do a salad, if you like."

"Right." I took up a knife and started slicing and cutting with more enthusiasm than talent.

It was worth it. Clare said, when she'd finished eating: "That was really marvelous. I don't know when I've had such a lovely meal." She also insisted that we all three do the washing-up. When it was done, my mother said:

"Why don't you two go up to Mel's room for a bit?"

I could cheerfully have strangled her. That was what she used to say when I had friends round for tea when I was eight. Clare was a grown woman. She might want to make grown-up conversation with my mother and me in the lounge. I was just trying to think of a way of telling my mother this tactfully (when what I really wanted to do was yell at her), when Clare said:

"Yes, Mel, do show me. I love looking at people's rooms. You've seen mine."

"It's nothing like yours, I'm afraid," I said, leading the way up the stairs. "It's a bit of a mess."

Does everyone say that when they show someone their room for the first time? It's a remark that seems to pop out by itself, whether there's any truth in the statement or not. The fact was, I'd spent hours arranging it in the way I thought would be most Clare-like. I'd hidden all my cuddly toys in the bottom of my cupboard, taken down pictures of such pop stars as I thought she might disapprove of, and moved my babyish books to the very top shelf of my bookcase. I'd pushed dolls into the space between the desk and the bed.

"What a lovely room!" said Clare, going over to the window and looking out. "I like your monkey-puzzle tree." She turned to face me, and grinned. "I see you've put your dolls where I can't see them."

"How did you know?"

"Everyone does it. I do it. When I first met Philip— that's my ex-husband—I was your age, and honestly, I put almost as much time into fixing up my room for his approval as I do now designing a set."

I giggled. "I give up. Next time you come, they'll all be out again, I promise you. I don't know why I hid them. I suppose I wanted to look grown-up."

"I can't think why," Clare said. "Nothing so terrific about being grown-up. I wouldn't rush into it, if I were you. I did. It's a mistake."

"Marrying so young, do you mean?"

"I suppose I do mean that. I don't know." Clare came over to the window and looked out at the garden. Then she turned to me.

"I know you ought not to make up rules for people. I know that everyone's different, but still, I don't think it's a good idea to marry young. I wouldn't recommend it. You expect all the wrong things."

"How do you mean?"

"I think I thought," Clare said, "that I would lead the life of a doll in a dolls' house. Do you understand? Make everything neat and pretty. Set up a little home with curtains at the windows and carpets on the floor, and all would be well. It was a good game for a bit, but it wasn't a life, not really. Not for real people. Real people need to get out, move about, have a bit of freedom, go here, there, and everywhere. At least for a while."

"Is that why you left? Because you'd got fed up with staying home and keeping house . . . like a doll-wife?"

"Not really, no," Clare smiled. "Oh, it's true, I *was* getting fed up, and probably I wouldn't have stood it forever, but Daddy Doll beat me to it."

I must have looked shocked, because Clare said: "Don't look so agonized, Mel. It was to be expected, I suppose. I don't think anyone should settle down at nineteen years old, do you? We were foolish to try. I can see that now, but it's difficult to be reasonable and sensible when you're madly in love. It's a great pity, really. A kind of design-fault in most people, I always think. In comes passionate love, and out goes common sense."

"But you still haven't said what happened. To you and Philip, I mean."

"He met someone else. He fell in love with her. He was very honest about it. There was no deception, and I thank him for that. I couldn't have borne being lied to." She shook her head. "I haven't really spoken about it to anyone except my family before. I hope you don't mind."

"No." I couldn't find the right words. Everything I

wanted to say sounded pompous. "I'm glad you told me. It makes me feel . . . honored."

"Probably," said Clare, "it's because you remind me of my sister. I've got a sister about your age . . . maybe a bit older, and before I left home I used to tell her everything, and now I don't see her nearly often enough."

"I'm an only child," I said. I wanted to tell her about the thousands of pretend games I'd played when I was younger, in which an older sister had had a starring role, but I didn't. Instead I said: "It's quite boring. You have to keep having conversations with yourself."

"Those are the best kind," Clare smiled. "No possible quarrels."

"But predictable," I said. "Amazingly predictable."

For some reason, this struck us as tremendously funny, and we both started laughing uncontrollably, until my mother shouted up to us to come and have a cup of coffee.

Sometimes, when I'm bored with my fantasy about being on a desert island, I pretend instead that I'm on a stage and that this room is a set. Over there, instead of the wall, the acting area ends and the audience begins. To the left, there are bookshelves, to the right, some chairs and a table, and I am upstage, next to a beautifully painted piece of scenery: a window with a view onto the street, partly blocked by the huge, overstated, jungle leaves of a castor-oil tree. Anyone who walks into this set sits downstage right to talk to me. They bring me the threads of what is happening in the world outside and I put them together into passable imitations of the fabric of real life.

On the Tuesday after the auditions, when I got to the Project, I noticed that some men had started work on the wasteland in front of the theater. I was early and the weather was dry, so I stood and watched for a while to see if I could spot any pattern or order in their work. I gave up almost at once. All they seemed to be doing was digging holes in all kinds of places, and putting sticks into the ground and tying bright orange plastic ribbons between one stick and the next. I could make no sense at all of what was going on, so I walked on, and in through the Stage Door and said good morning to George, feeling the pleasant glow of being practically a real live professional actress. Belonging. I could hardly believe it was really me, really on my way to rehearsal.

The first thing we all had to do that morning was crowd into Chris's little office and look at the model of the set, while he explained to us that here, on these chairs and this sofa, was where the sisters would be talking at the beginning of Act One, and through this false archway, a little to the left and upstage, that's where the birthday table would be set, and all the eating and drinking would go on. The model was divided into four, like the ground floor of a dolls' house with the outside walls and the roof removed. There was one room for each act: the Prozorovs' garden for Act Four had tiny little wooden seats, the outside of the house and even the beginnings of the avenue of firs and overhanging branches of the maple tree just visible in the corner. The lounge in Act Two was the same room as in Act One, but a dark and wintry version of it. Evidently the sisters put away the light rugs and pale green flowery curtains at the end of the summer, and brought out heavier furnishings, to protect themselves from the cold of a Northern Russian winter. They were intent (until the coming of Natasha into the household, at any rate) to keep things the way they had been in Old Basmannaya Street, long ago when their mother was alive. Clare had made little lamps, and potted plants and miniature cushions and pictures in gilded frames. I couldn't stop looking. I was the last person out of the office, so caught up was I in admiring the screen that separated Olga's bed and Irina's in the Act Three set. It was made from varnished matchsticks and paper doilies.

"It's beautiful, isn't it?" Chris said. "Exactly like lace."

"Yes," I said. "The whole thing's marvelous. I've been longing to see it. I can't believe Clare made it all by herself."

"Every bit."

"I think that's amazing."

"We're lucky, aren't we?" Chris grinned. "Tell you what though, I wanted to talk to you—to ask you if you'd be willing to be a sort of general understudy for them: all three of the sisters, I mean."

"Understudy? You mean, go on for them if they're ill or something? Learn their words?"

"Well, yes, I'm afraid so . . . that's what I wanted to ask you. Are you a quick study?"

A lunatic vision of a book-lined room on wheels flashed into my head. I said:

"I'm quick at learning things by heart—do you mean that?"

"Yes, I do. Will you do it?"

"Oh, yes please," I said.

"Great." Chris said. "We'll tell them all at rehearsal. Come on, we'd better get going."

I floated happily behind him up to the Rehearsal Room. Who's Teacher's Pet, now then, eh? Term hardly started and already promoted to the status of a monitor . . . understudy. In the kind of movies my mother goes in for, that is Theatrical Cliché Number Two. The understudy takes over the main part and is hailed as a shining new star. And Theatrical Cliché Number One? That's when the theater falls down/blows up or is otherwise put out of action and Our Resourceful Heroine and Hero, standing in the school canteen, the local police station, a department store—

anywhere, really—say, with a look of utter astonishment and wonder on their faces:

"Let's do the show right here!" almost as if those words had never been spoken before.

By the time we'd reached the Rehearsal Room, I'd stopped feeling euphoric and panic had set in. It was quite true. I do have a good memory, and I knew I could get the words of a pop song by heart in two seconds flat, but Olga, Masha, *and* Irina? Wasn't that rather a lot? I sighed. There wasn't going to be much free time from now on, that was for damn sure.

"Right," Chris said when we'd all settled down. "You've read the play to yourselves and we've read it through together. What do you think of it?"

Silence. No one wanted to be the first to speak. At last, Simon, the small, blond, puppylike boy playing Baron Tusenbach, said:

"It hasn't got a lot of action, has it? I mean, not very much happens, does it? There's a lot of talking and . . . and that's about it."

I was sitting next to Roland Sweet. He seemed to be older than the rest of us: in his twenties, even, like Chris, but perhaps that was just because he was so chubby. He leaned over to me and whispered:

"What does he expect, then? *The Texas Chainsaw Massacre?*"

I giggled quietly. Mike had taken up Simon's objection and was saying, quite vehemently:

"That's crap . . . just because people aren't swashing and buckling and fainting and things all over the place, that doesn't mean there's no action. I mean, look what happens to them all. Masha loves Vershinin, who is married, and loses him and has to stay with Kulygin, her husband, whom

54

she doesn't really love. Tusenbach loves Irina and dies, Natasha transforms the house and the master of the house to suit her pretty little ideas of what's right and proper, and gets her revenge on the three sisters who look down on her at the beginning of the play. Olga becomes headmistress. Irina grows up. The avenue of firs is going to be cut down . . ." Mike stopped speaking quite abruptly, as though he had suddenly realized how carried away he was getting.

"I agree with Mike," Chris said. "I think a tremendous amount happens. What do you all think the play's about?"

Andrew, sitting next to Louise, put his hand up.

"Yes," Chris smiled. "You don't actually have to put your hand up . . . it's not school." (Laughter.)

Andrew blushed and spoke directly to his trainers. "I think it's about exile. About people being away from home. All the soldiers are in a barracks in this grotty little town miles from anywhere, the sisters are supposed to be in Moscow, but they're not, and they're kind of homeless twice over, because of Natasha, who makes them share a room and changes everything in their house around to suit herself. Even their brother."

"And the birds are flying south at the end," Louise said. "They are looking for a home, too, in a way."

Dinah said: "I think it's about people doing things they never meant to do. Like Olga being a headmistress even though she never really wanted to, Irina working in the Post Office, and brother Andrey, who's supposed to be the brilliant one, getting all fat and lazy and in debt and gambling and everything, and ending up pushing a pram around the garden."

"That's right," Chris said. "And it's not only that they're doing things they never intended, it's also that Chekhov seems to be saying that *all* their endeavors are absurd in a

55

way, and that in the end nothing matters. You should try," he looked directly at Dinah and smiled and she dimpled back at him and (I swear) fluttered her eyelashes, "counting the number of times someone in the play says: 'It doesn't matter.' It's like a chorus, running right through." (Smile, dimple, flutter once again.) I chipped into the idyll at this point to say that what struck me was that, apart from Irina at the beginning of the play (for about five seconds and on her name day at that!), nobody ever says they're happy or is at all aware of happiness. Andrey even says: *"The present is loathsome."* They've all *been* happy in the past and they're all sure they *will be* happy in the future, if they can get to Moscow/work/get over this bad patch, etc., etc. Except for Natasha, they're all either lookers-back or lookers-forward, or both. And Natasha, for all her faults, does at least go ahead and do what makes her happy.

"But she does it," said Charlie Mitchell, who was playing Ferapont and who had a clown's sad and funny face, "at other people's expense. She's selfish. She makes Olga and Irina squash up in one room, Sofochka, her little daughter, is going to be moved into Andrey's study . . . everything that makes her happy is a destruction of other people's happiness."

We all agreed with Charlie about Natasha's selfish character.

"Right," said Chris. "I want Act One beginners on stage in fifteen minutes. Tricia, Louise, and Dinah, Mel here is going to be your understudy, so you won't have to worry if you suddenly get appendicitis or something."

All three of them smiled and said, "Great" and "Terrific," but I could see (just for a second behind their eyes and then it was gone) the thought forming: what if I fall ill and she turns out to be better than me? Clearly, Tricia,

Louise, and Dinah all decided instantly that I was no sort of competition at all, because they seemed genuinely pleased and we all trooped down to the Green Room together like bosom buddies.

The Green Room was an Elephant's Graveyard for sofas. It was where old sofas went to die. There were four of them altogether, squashed into a very small space. They were frayed and torn, with their springs and stuffing spilling out on to the floor, and they were uniformly wobbly and all groaned and creaked with pain when anyone sat down. Once upon a time, the square of something-or-other on the floor had probably been a carpet and a riot of color to boot, but both color and pattern had disappeared, and dim, ghostly shapes of woolly flowers were all that was left. A large part of the carpet was hidden under a low table, which took up most of the space between the sofas. There was a drinks machine in the corner, with a bit of a wonky aim, which spat khaki-colored liquid into (or around) white plastic cups. And above the door was the tannoy, a loudspeaker system which was constantly switched on so that you could hear every word said on stage and (theoretically, at least) listen for your cue. The Green Room was also, and perhaps most importantly, the home of Olly, the Project cat, called after Sir Laurence Olivier. He was fat and black and white and was supposed to be on the lookout for mice, but in fact spent his days curled up on one or another of the moribund sofas.

There was also a pay phone in one corner, nestling under a kind of plastic hood, which was supposed to provide soundproofing and didn't. I went over to it and dialed Mrs. Sandler's number. Clare answered almost at once.

"Clare? It's Mel. I'm ringing from the Green Room. Doesn't that sound glamorous and professional?"

57

"Yes . . . listen, I'm on my way in to the theater now. Is it anything urgent?"

"I just wanted to tell you that we've seen the set. It's fantastic. Unbelievable."

"That's what I love about you, Mel . . . you're such a mistress of understatement!"

"Rubbish. It's the literal truth. It's terrific. And it's not just me. Everyone thinks so. Chris thinks so, too."

"Tell me what he said."

"He said it was beautiful. He said we were lucky to have you."

"Bless you, Mel. You say all the right things. Listen, I'm coming in now. I'll see you. OK? How's Mike?"

"Which Mike?"

"Acting all innocent, are we? How many are there? The one in the cast. The one playing Vershinin. He's got his eye on you, from what I've seen."

"You hardly know him. I hardly know him. I hardly know anyone."

"Doesn't take long in the theater. See you in a minute, OK?"

"Yes, right," I said. "Bye." I put the phone down. Mike. I would have to ask Clare exactly what she meant when she arrived. Meanwhile what she had said gave me a small thrill each time I thought of it.

For the first couple of days, most of us sat in the auditorium during rehearsals, concentrating like mad, listening to every word, not wanting to miss anything, but after a while, most people (not me of course, I had four parts to learn, didn't I?) adopted a more relaxed attitude and brought in something to do during the long stretches of hanging about. Charlie brought in a couple of decks of cards and set up

58

a Poker Academy, where he and Andrew and Simon and Roland and Mike and sometimes even Ruth and Louise fooled around playing everything from Snap to Five Card Stud. Whenever Tricia or Dinah or Louise or I came into the room, they'd all hoot with laughter, the cardplayers, and Charlie would say in a genteel, Jean Brodie-ish sort of Scottish accent:

"Och, here's the ladies now and we should be changing to an elegant game of bridge, should we not?"

They all used to pretend that they were "below stairs" in the kitchen of the Prozorovs' house, and comment vulgarly on the high-flown sentiments they could hear coming to them over the tannoy. I enjoyed sitting in the Green Room, in spite of plastic cups standing around the table in small, khaki puddles, but most of the time I had to sit in the orchestra seats and pay close attention to what was going on, and I couldn't even do what Tricia and Louise both did and bring in some knitting. I developed, from watching them, a whole theory of Character Through Knitting. Louise had only just learned, you could tell. She was making a scarf (for Andrew?) on very large needles, using odd scraps of wool and doing the whole thing in garter stitch. Whenever she was called up onto the stage, she dug her fat, bright green needles into whichever ball of wool she happened to be using, and left the scarf hanging over the back of the seat, and trailing onto the floor, which was not the cleanest place in the world, in spite of George's best efforts.

Tricia, on the other hand, was making a jumper in a Fair Isle pattern using thin needles and wool in about a thousand different colors, all wound daintily on to small, plastic bobbins. When Chris called her, she would fold the whole lot away into a white cloth and lay it gently in a patchwork knitting bag. If Olga and Masha had been knitters, I thought the first time I saw them, they would each have worked in precisely these two styles.

Dinah had an endless supply of magazines and a portable laboratory of nail-beautifying equipment. She could spend twenty minutes on a nail: nail care as an Art Form, I suppose you could call it. Certainly her nails were very pretty at the end of the treatment and I suppose it passed the time quite harmlessly.

I spent a great deal of my time watching Chris in action. I'd never seen any real-live directing before, but had evolved a mixed-up kind of fantasy of a power-mad figure in a canvas chair with his name stenciled on it. Chris couldn't have been more different. For one thing, he hardly ever raised his voice. Instructions, when he gave them, were spoken softly for the most part. He indicated more or less where we were to move to, sit, stand, and so on, but he always consulted the actors:

"Mike, what about trying that speech standing with your back to Louise? How does that feel? Sort of speaking over your shoulder?"

or:

"Mel, you're dead embarrassed, OK? Can you blush? Think of something absolutely horrible, something that makes you cringe inside . . ."

or:

"Dinah, I don't think a smile there, do you? Or perhaps just an inward-turning private smile. What do you think she's feeling just there? Can you tell me?"

or:

"Charlie, OK, Ferapont's a bit of comic relief, but I don't think the whole Goon Show rolled into one. Try one Goon at a time and see which is best. Or, how's this, Charlie, a whole new funny voice all your own . . ."

Chris also appeared to be endlessly patient. He actively encouraged the company to come to him with problems, and come they did:

"Chris, I don't know what this speech is supposed to mean . . . I can't say that and walk around the table at the same time . . . Do I go through this door . . . Is it a window . . . Sorry, thought it was a door . . . Do I love my husband at all? . . . Did I once? Is it all right to go down here? . . . Can you still see me if I sit, or does Louise hide me? . . . Is Masha guilty about her love for Vershinin? Does Olga envy her sisters? . . . Where is the screen going to be? . . . Where is Solyony standing when I say this? . . ." On and on *ad infinitum*. What would happen when there were lighting plans, costumes, and scenery to deal with? I dreaded to think, but Chris seemed unflappable, and little by little we all calmed down in his presence and approached most rehearsals in a somewhat quieter spirit.

The one great advantage of spending the better part of the day in the third row of the orchestra was that everyone who came in for any length of time at all seemed to sit down next to me, and in the half darkness I learned an awful lot about everyone in little snatches of whispered conversation. It did occur to me that I should set myself up as a one-woman computer dating service, or at least some kind of counselor, full of good advice for the lovelorn, because what struck me (listening to the whispers with one ear and trying to keep track of what was going on on stage with the other) was:

a) everybody fancied someone who didn't fancy them.

b) everybody was being fancied by someone they didn't fancy at all.

Tra, la, la! *Midsummer Night's Dream* all over again . . . and virtually every love story in the world. I fail to see why the whole business has to be so complicated. In any case,

61

by the end of the first week, I had a pattern as intricate as a square dance in my head. Louise, for instance, was devoted to Andrew, of course, and had been since primary school, but she also told me in confidence that Andrew was getting a bit . . . well . . . boring would be putting it a bit strongly . . . a bit predictable, and she definitely felt like something more exciting. She had settled on Mike, with Matt as second choice.

"I think," she whispered to me one day, "Mike's really gorgeous. I've always thought so. He goes to our school and if it wasn't for the fact that Andrew would throw a wobbler . . . well . . ." She shook her head.

"But you and Andrew have been going out together for ages."

"We have. I feel like bloody Darby and Joan and that's the truth. Eleven years! Can you imagine? I mean, most marriages don't even last that long, do they?"

I thought of Clare. "No. No, they don't."

"There's nothing wrong with Andrew," Louise continued. "I don't want you to think that. He's kind and good to me and everything . . . and he does love me, only . . ."

"What?"

"I dunno. He's not very . . ." She blushed and whispered even more quietly. "You know . . . he doesn't go in for a lot of kissing and things like that, and I . . ." She slid into silence.

"You'd like there to be more of that sort of thing?"

"Yes," Louise said, "I would, only I don't know if I'd like it with Andrew. I mean, I know him so well, all the novelty's sort of worn off. The excitement's not there. D'you know what I mean?" She sighed. "Pity about Mike. I really like him. He's so . . . quiet and mysterious. No one knows anything about him really, even though he's ever so friendly. It's a shame."

"What's a shame?"

"Don't you know? Crikey, not got eyes in your head, you haven't, if you can't see he's after you."

"Me?"

"Yes, dear. You. Haven't you seen the way he looks at you? You should thank your lucky stars I'm not jealous of you. Too nice, that's me. Too friendly. I'll have to settle for Matt." She winked at me and grinned in the half-light.

Louise was right, of course. I *had* noticed, although I didn't tell her so.

Clare had also mentioned it again. One day, we were sitting together in the orchestra during a rehearsal of Act One.

"Can you see?" said Clare. "Whenever he's not speaking, he's looking into the auditorium to see if you're there."

"How do you know it's me he's looking for?"

"I do, that's all. Don't you? I saw him the other day, too, in the Green Room. He came in, looked all around at everybody and then as soon as he caught sight of you, he stopped looking and went and sat down beside you. Remember?"

"Yes, but that was probably just a coincidence."

"Coincidence, my foot. Look at him now."

Mike had been swapping reminiscences about Moscow with Olga, and he'd got all mixed up with the Russian names. Nemetzkaya Street, he was supposed to say, and the Krasny barracks, and everything came out upside down. Everyone laughed, but Chris was quite annoyed.

"Oh, for heaven's sake," he said, "can't you even concentrate for five minutes? What is it out there that's so interesting anyway?"

Clare and I giggled and Mike blushed to the roots of his hair and said only: "Sorry, Chris."

"Right," Chris said, "now I don't care if it's Marilyn

Monroe in the audience, you're all to exist only in this small space. Not one bit of you is to be dissipated out there, get it?"

Everyone on stage nodded like good children.

"Don't you love Chris when he gets all tough like that?" I asked Clare.

She smiled. "I don't know. In a way, I suppose. I'm not seeing too much of him these days, what with rehearsals and everything, and I've got to go down to London on Thursday as well. We haven't had a chance to be alone together for ages."

She was looking down as she said this, doodling on a pad in the dim light that fell from the stage. She was frowning.

"I think," she said in the end, "there are some things we still haven't talked about."

I was just about to ask what things, when I had to go on stage. Perhaps, I reflected, Clare wouldn't want to tell me. I didn't like gossiping about my feelings, not even to Clare, especially as I wasn't yet sure that what I felt about Mike counted as "feelings" at all. I liked him, or thought I could like him, but the truth of the matter was, he was difficult to get to know. It wasn't that he was shy. It was perfectly easy to talk to him, he'd laugh and chat and gossip away about everyone, but he never, ever, said one word about himself or his family or his home. For a long time, I didn't know where he lived. To begin with, he never invited me out, not even to the good old Capricorn Café, not even to go Dutch, and this was because we always went there after rehearsals finished at five o'clock for a quick cup of coffee with froth on top, and Mike always rushed off home the moment he got out of the theater. It was a mystery and we wondered about it quite a lot behind the steamed-up windows of the Capricorn.

"I think," said Tricia, "that he comes from one of those

orphanage places, and they only let him out for certain hours and then he has to be back."

"Or," said Matt, "his mother's an alcoholic and he has to rush back and see she hasn't harmed herself while he's been away. I saw a movie like that once, where this guy had to keep fishing his boozed-up mother out of the bath. Anyway, Louise, you and Andrew ought to know. I mean, you go to the same school and everything, don't you?"

Louise looked sharply at him.

"You got the addresses and life histories of all your classmates then, have you?" She sipped her coffee haughtily.

"Anyway, he's not in our class." She smiled. "He fancies Mel, though. Bet Mel gets to know before anyone."

"And you needn't ask me," Andrew put in. "I only see him at Drama Club anyway."

"I suppose," Simon said, "we could always ask him."

"I have asked him," Ruth said, "and he always tries to wriggle out of it in one way or another. I think he just enjoys being enigmatic."

I said nothing during these conversations, because I thought that Mike may have been hiding something specifically from me rather than generally from the whole company and that could only mean one thing: he thought that I would like him less if I knew all about him. I resolved to keep quiet and reserve my judgment instead of opening my mouth and putting my foot in it.

Tricia said: "Mel, are you coming over to my house tonight, to go over Act Two?"

"Yes, I think so," I said and began scrabbling about in my bag, thinking to find my address book and check with Tricia about buses, ways of getting there, etc., etc., and that was when I noticed my copy of the play was missing. I swore loudly.

"I've got to go back to the theater. I've left my copy in the Green Room. Come on, Tricia, let's check this address." I wrote the bus numbers down in my notebook, pushed it back into my bag, and slipped out into the rain. It always seemed to be raining this past summer. I picked my way across the wet stony ground, hoping the theater would still be open.

"You're all right, Miss," George said. "If you wipe your feet. There's still a few of them about, mucking around with lights and such." He sighed. "I can remember blue and orange footlights, you know. Lovely, they were. Blue and orange. Squares of light all along the front of the stage. Smashing."

"I've only come to get my copy. I think I left it in the Green Room. I won't be a second."

I reflected, walking along the passage to the Green Room, that really, theaters and schools *did* have a lot in common. In this case, it was the feeling of both places when they were empty. When everyone had gone home, they were both still haunted in a strange way by voices, words, plenty going on—lots of busyness and rushing around suddenly gone. They both had an echoey kind of silence about them.

At five-thirty or so on an August afternoon, there should have been a little bit of light coming through the small, grubby window, but it wasn't (what with the rain and everything) enough to see by, so I switched the lights on to look for my copy of the play. I saw it at once, on one of the sofas. I also saw that Charlie had left the cards (typically) in grave danger of being soaked by an encroaching tea-puddle, so I felt I had to move them and put them in a tidy pile. Then, I thought, I might as well wipe up the mess or we'll all have to sit here looking at it tomorrow morning, so I hunted about for a suitable cloth. As I wiped,

I realized that the tannoy hadn't been switched off. I could hear that there was someone . . . some people still on stage. It wasn't an extra rehearsal, because whoever was there wasn't speaking loudly enough for me to catch the words. What it sounded like to me was a murmur.

Now, I suppose you could argue that I should have switched off the light, shut the Green Room door, and marched firmly out of the theater. Perhaps I should have, but I felt I simply had to know what was going on on stage, just to satisfy my own curiosity, and furthermore (I said to myself in justification as I crept down to the prompt corner where Janet usually sat on a high chair), if this conversation was going on onstage, there couldn't be much about it that was a deadly secret. After all, anyone could walk in at any time, as I was doing, even though I had no intention of being seen. I had a good idea, of course, even before I saw them sitting together on the Prozorovs' chaise lounge, of who it was I'd find. Dinah and Chris. Fortunately, they had their backs to me. Still, the chaise lounge was very close indeed to the prompt corner, so I shrank back into the shadows by Janet's chair and listened to what was going on. It soon became clear that Chris was in the process of reassuring Dinah about the quality of her acting performance. She was expressing doubt, uncertainty, fear, hesitation: you name it and she was expressing it. Like mad and with a great many attendant sighs and heavings of her delicate bosom. She said:

"Sometimes I lie in bed at night and all the words just go tumbling through my head and I can't sleep for worrying. I don't know whether . . ."

"Oh, Dinah" (this was Chris, sounding a little out of breath), "you mustn't worry, honestly, love. You'll be so good . . . I know you will. Look, I'll tell you what. Why don't we have a few sessions just the two of us. I'll go through all of your scenes with you, slowly and carefully, and then you'll feel much more confident, I'm sure."

"Oh, Chris, really? Are you sure you don't mind? You're so busy . . . I know how busy you are . . ." The voices were fading away. Perhaps they had moved off the chaise lounge. I couldn't see the two of them, but I could well imagine Dinah gazing up at him, lips parted and coated with gloss like the lips pasted up all over her walls, eyes beaming away like headlights: adoration, adoration, adoration. An ominous silence followed. I sat near Janet's chair and trembled. How long could I sit there and not look? I couldn't bear the suspense. In the end, I peeked. Chris and Dinah had indeed stood up and were now right at the edge of the stage, standing very close to one another. I thought (I couldn't be sure) that he had just stroked the top of her head. I knew I had to get out of there fast, but I couldn't risk making a noise. I'd have to wait until they'd gone. I heard Chris say: "Thursday, then. 'Bye, love," and then Dinah rushed straight past my hiding place without seeing me. She was quite clearly walking on air. I stood in the dark for ten minutes to give her time to get away from the theater, and in that time, one thought filled my mind: Clare was going down to London on Thursday and staying overnight with her parents. She had told me so on Sunday night.

Eighty-seven different ways of dealing with what I'd seen on the stage that night occurred to me within the first few minutes of seeing it. I was still weighing them all up the next day when I arrived at the theater, but I'd almost decided to do nothing on the grounds that what I'd seen hadn't been very much after all, only a good director saying he'd give a little bit of extra help to a conscientious and ambitious actress. How could I tell anyone about that and make something of it? I couldn't do all the sighing, eyelash fluttering, and bosom heaving to convey to people the added dimension that I'd felt in the conversation.

I decided to wait and see what happened. Clare had said, only the other day, that she hadn't made up her mind about Chris, felt unwilling to commit herself ... well, maybe Chris had given up the pursuit and was going for someone who was obviously goggle-eyed about him. Maybe he'd even told Clare how he felt about Dinah. How *did* he feel about Dinah? How did Dinah feel about him? Was it anything to do with me? Since when had I appointed myself guardian of Clare's thin skin? She was supposed to be grown-up, after all, and I was only . . . only what? I refused to think of myself as a child.

I wasn't needed for the first rehearsal that morning, so I decided to go and have a cup of coffee with Ruby, the wardrobe mistress, and her friend Joyce, who worked in the Box Office. I'd met these two ladies while helping Clare one day. We'd been carting boxes of old uniforms from other shows up to Ruby's lair on the third floor and the coffee and chat was so pleasant when we got there that I'd felt instantly at home, snug in the smell of the steam iron and the damp clothes. On this particular morning I didn't even have to put the kettle on.

"Come in, love," said Ruby when she saw me. "We've just made a cup, haven't we, Joyce. I daresay the kettle's still hot." I made my coffee and then pretended to be looking for something in a cupboard. Joyce was saying:

"It beats me, Ruby, it really does, how you manage." She shifted her heavy body into a more comfortable position in the canvas chair and dipped her Rich Tea biscuit into her cup. She turned to me.

"I was just remarking to Ruby, I could no more do all the sewing and washing and ironing and cleaning and sorting and folding and dyeing and whatnot that she does than fly to the moon."

"Well," said Ruby, coming up for air from the bottom of an enormous wicker bin in which she'd been rummaging, "we all do what we can, don't we? You sort out all those tickets and money and things. I've spent my whole life with clothes, one way and another, first being a machinist in the factory, then married with three daughters and a husband who needed a clean white shirt every day of his life."

She laughed. "I tell you, you don't know what ironing is, or washing or starching until you've had three daughters and a fussy man to attend to . . . the average production's a lot less work. With some of those modern-type plays, you hardly have any work at all: some playwrights'll put the cast in sand up to their necks, or else it's jeans and T-shirts for everybody. I'll tell you the truth, Joyce, but don't spread it about too much . . . I'm quite looking forward to this *Three Sisters*. Lovely long dresses, uniforms, ribbons . . . oh, it'll be grand. That Clare'll do it a treat, I know she will."

Joyce ran a hand over her corrugated-iron waves and took another biscuit. "She's a sweetie, that Clare, isn't she? So dainty. Poor thing . . . that young and already divorced. They do say, don't they, that he left her for an older woman. I don't know what the world's coming to, I don't really. But it seems to me that she and our young Chris are seeing rather a lot of each other."

Ruby snorted with laughter. "They're only young once, aren't they? I say the best of British luck to them. I reckon they should see as much of each other as they can—know what I mean?"

Joyce coughed and wrinkled her nose with distaste at Ruby's vulgarity. Ruby went on rummaging in the bin. Joyce said:

"Well, they do look good together, I will say that. He's what I call a really good-looking young man. I saw them at the bus stop once . . . kissing, they were. I could have been on another planet for all the notice they took of me. I hope," Joyce continued, "that that young woman knows what she's about. Our Chris looks to me like . . ." She searched for the right word, ". . . a bit of a Don Juan."

"Nonsense," Ruby said firmly. "He's been here two years and I've certainly never seen him so besotted."

71

"Besotted can get unbesotted," Joyce said darkly. "Besotted can burn itself out. I hope that nice young Clare's prepared."

"You never are, though, are you?" said Ruby sagely. "However much you tell yourself you are, it never works, does it?"

"Exactly," said Joyce. "That's exactly what I mean. Now I'll just have one more biscuit and then I must fly down to the Box Office and sort out the season tickets for next year."

After Joyce had left, I finished my coffee and chatted to Ruby for a while about the proper way of tying a lace square around one's neck. Then I went down to the Green Room. What I really needed was someone to talk to. Someone who would help me sort it all out, see it in perspective, someone who would tell me that it wasn't my business and that it was only by chance I'd come across Chris and Dinah on the stage together, someone who would tell me to forget the whole thing. I sat down next to Olly who was cat-snoozing on the greenish sofa. Bits of the play came floating into the room over the tannoy, crackling and echoey and disembodied as if they came from very far away. But perhaps I was the one: the action on the stage was where things really were, and I was the one who was far away. Roland was saying:

"*It's two years since I last went on a spree . . . what does it matter?*" Andrew's voice: "*A teacher's what I am . . .*" Dinah said: "*Masha's out of sorts today,*" and a little time later: "*Please don't talk to me about love . . .*" and Simon said: "*What are you thinking about?*" and Dinah answered: "*You say that life is beautiful. For the three of us, for me and my sisters, life hasn't been beautiful up to now . . . it's choked us like weeds.*" Those words were

72

my cue. I was on in about ten seconds. I leapt to my feet and fled down the corridor to the stage, racing to be in the Prompt Corner before my entrance. As I left the Green Room, I could hear Janet calling me over the tannoy:

"Mel, onstage now please. Mel, on stage."

I rushed on and spoke the first words: *"They're sitting down to lunch already . . . I'm late."*

Chris laughed. "Stop, Mel! I've heard of acting but this is ridiculous. You're late, OK, but you have not just run the Boston Marathon. Flustered, yes. Out of breath and red in the face, definitely not. OK? Try again."

I went off, composed myself, and came on again a little more demurely, doing my best to imagine I was wearing a pink dress with (horror of horrors, according to Olga, Masha, and Irina) a green belt. Yuck!

I could see Mike standing in the wings on the other side of the stage. He was waiting there because he knew I had to come off on that side after kissing Andrey. This was a bit of the play I always dreaded, and it wasn't helped by Mike staring at me every time. Kissing someone in cold blood like that is extremely difficult. I don't know how film stars manage . . . perhaps there are certain tricks and techniques you can learn to make it appear convincing. I mean, it wasn't that I disliked Matt or anything, but to stand there in front of all those people and open your mouth and have some person just go banging their teeth against yours any old how they fancied . . . it made me feel stupid. Chris said: "We'll work on that next time, you two. We always leave it too late." He laughed. "Mel, you must at least *try* and look as if you're enjoying it, you know. I mean, at the very least you shouldn't have clenched fists, you know, not in a passionate embrace." I looked down and sure enough, my fists were bunched up like a boxer's.

Everyone laughed. Except Mike. The fact that he wasn't giggling like the rest of them made me go up to him in the wings on the way out.

"Can I talk to you, Mike? Now, this lunchtime? Can we go for a walk or something?"

"Yes, sure. Is anything wrong?"

"I want to ask your advice about something."

"OK. I'll see you in about two minutes in front of the theater. I've got to get something from the Rehearsal Room."

In the Green Room, Louise said:

"Coming to the Capricorn for lunch?"

"No, I'm going for a walk with Mike."

"Ooh," she said, "like that, is it?"

I'd had enough by that time. I yelled: "No, it bloody isn't like that," over my shoulder at her.

"Temper, temper," she said, quite sunnily.

I stormed out of the theater in a rage. Honestly, I thought, all this love stuff would be a whole lot easier if people didn't giggle and wink and poke their fingers at you. All you had to do was like someone a bit and you were fair game for any amount of teasing, rib-tickling, and wink-wink-nudge-nudgery. People didn't take it seriously enough. Or perhaps it really was all a huge joke and I was a fool to be worrying about it so. After all, was it any of my business if Chris was now about to leave Clare for Dinah? I couldn't do anything to prevent it. Why should I bother? Why should I care about Clare's feelings? And Dinah? I'd never even met her till about two weeks ago— why should it be any business of mine if she wished to behave like a character from a soap opera?

I was leaning against the dustbins thinking all this when

Mike appeared. He shook his finger at me and said in his best George voice:

"Those aren't just any old dustbins, you know. Those dustbins have appeared on stage in many a production of whatever that play's called with folk in dustbins on stage. There've been some well-known actors in them bins, I'd have you know." He changed to his own voice. "Are you OK? You look a bit funny."

"Mike, you've got to listen to this. It's going to sound stupid. Are you ready?"

"I'm ready. Where're we going?"

"That way," I said and strode off ahead of him across the builders' wasteland toward a chewed-up-looking square of grass a few hundred yards away, laughingly known as "The Park."

I was surprised, when I did tell Mike the whole story, to see what a short time it took—a couple of minutes, that was all.

"That's it," I said. "I'm sorry I dragged you off out here just for this silly little five minutes' worth, but it's been filling my head so much, it's kind of grown out of all proportion. It sounds trivial when I tell it to you as well. Silly."

"That's because," Mike said, "it's happening to other people. It's easy to say that other people's problems are unimportant, but they're very important to them. The point is that if Clare likes Chris even a bit, she's going to be hurt. If Chris likes Clare even a bit, he's going to feel guilty, and they'll both feel worse if Clare finds out by accident in some way." He thought for a moment. "The best thing would be for Chris to come clean. Tell her. If there's anything to tell. Look, neither of us knows Chris well enough to tackle him, but can't you have a word with Dinah? Find out what's going on ... maybe she could persuade Chris to tell Clare."

"But today's Thursday already. She's having that extra rehearsal tonight, after the ordinary rehearsal's finished. I can't speak to her tonight."

"Tomorrow morning, then ... what about that?"

"OK," I said. "I'll try. I suppose she's the only one I can speak to, really. What'll I say?"

"Don't worry about that now. We've got to get back to the theater or we'll be late." Mike stood up and took my hand to pull me to my feet. Then, as we walked back past the gaping houses, he kept on holding my hand in his and I found it felt good, safe and warm, like being a child again. I was sorry, in a way, that we'd had to spend the time talking about other people when I could have been finding out more about Mike, and I thought of saying something as we walked, but we were striding along much too quickly for an intimate chat, and besides, I thought there was a chance that Mike would let go of my hand, if I reminded him too forcefully of my presence.

That evening, rehearsals finished at five o'clock and I went to the Capricorn with Roland and Tricia.

"I won't have anything to eat, though," I said. "My mother'll have supper ready for me."

"So will mine, duckie, so will mine," said Roland, patting his rather bulging shirt front, "but that's not going to stop me indulging in a really unscrupulous cream cake. I've been thinking of little else all afternoon."

Tricia laughed. "So that's what the Doctor is thinking about, is it, as he sits on that sofa on stage, stroking his imaginary beard. You're supposed to be thinking very profound and meaningful things, aren't you?"

"Not really," said Roland, biting into an éclair. "You can think what you like as long as you come in on your cue properly. You forget, little chickens, that your Uncle Roland is a good deal older than you."

"How old?" I asked.

"Twenty," answered Roland, "—going on fifty-six. It comes of being the youngest child of very frail parents in a rather posh suburb, who look at my stomach and think (quite rightly in all probability), 'With a stomach like that, the lad could be a stockbroker.' They cannot understand this mumming, this prancing about on a stage, this lust for the limelight. I mean, to them, theater people are not a very long way away from criminals. You know: immoral, gypsy-like, dangerous—definitely part of a kind of underworld."

"My mum and dad are a bit like that," said Tricia. "Well, not quite as bad. I don't think they think much about the theater at all . . . or acting. Even the stuff on TV . . . well, they know it's people acting, really, only they deliberately forget and then they can believe in things more, d'you know what I mean?"

I nodded. "Lots of people are like that. Sending baby clothes to imaginary babies."

Roland had finished his éclair and was looking out of the window. It was steamed up, as usual, so he'd rubbed himself a small porthole and was eyeing the street with interest. "Now there," he said, "is a turnup for the proverbial book, darlings, only don't say I said it."

"Who is it?" Tricia and I both leaned forward to have a look. Charlie and Ruth were walking to the bus stop. They were holding hands. Their heads were close together. Roland began to trill in a high, falsetto voice:

"It was a lover and his lass,
With a heigh and a ho,

77

And a heigh nonny no . . ."

"Belt up," said Tricia. "You're showing us up."

"Well," said Roland, "that's interesting. And I thought young Ruth, who's a dark sort of quietish horse, was taken with Matt."

"You're behind the times," Tricia said. "I saw Matt chatting up Louise yesterday. It looked quite . . . well, quite intense . . . more than just an ordinary conversation."

"And what about Andrew? Is he aware or unaware?" Roland said. "I must say, I find it hard to keep track of all these amorous vagaries among the young. Do I gather, for instance, that our beloved director is in the process of having his head turned by the delicious Irina?"

Tricia giggled. "Yeah, it's as good as a soap opera. It is, honestly."

I said, rather grimly: "It's not funny. Clare's being deceived. I don't actually think it's something to giggle about. Think how Clare feels."

"You're probably quite right," said Roland. "Slaps on the hand for Roland and Tricia. No, seriously, I'm sorry, only that's the thing about love, isn't it? It's so serious for the people involved—an absolute tragedy, or it can be, while for the rest of us, the lookers-on, well, honestly, it's like nothing so much as a Whitehall farce." Roland sniffed. "One is much safer," he said, "bestowing one's affections on luscious things to eat."

"But love is more slimming," said Tricia. "Some people go off their food completely."

"How awful," said Roland. "It doesn't bear thinking about."

"I've got to go home," I said. "Or I'll miss my food."

"Excuses, excuses," said Tricia. "You're only going because we were about to start asking about you and Mike."

I stood up and stuck my tongue out at them. "Tough.

Now I'm going to leave you here together for all the gossip-mongers to spot. By tomorrow, everyone will be drawing 'Roland loves Tricia' in little hearts all over every lamp-post."

"We are not ashamed," Roland declaimed to the entire café. "Our love dares to speak its name!"

Tricia blushed. "Honestly, Roland, shut up. You're a positive embarrassment."

"But you love me."

"I suppose so. Only shut up."

"Bye," I said.

"Mmm," said Roland and Tricia. They had embarked upon a serious kiss and both waved at me as I left the café. I felt a little envious of their pleasant and lighthearted relationship. Wouldn't it be fun, I thought, if love could always be like that, straightforward fun, like, well, rather like eating?

As I crossed the road to the bus stop, I saw Mike walking along the pavement toward the shops carrying a basket and looking down at his feet.

"Hello," I said, as he nearly bumped into me. He looked up, saw me, and blushed. Why? I wondered.

"Hi," he said. "I didn't expect to see you. I thought you'd be at home by now?"

"I was at the Capricorn with Roland and Tricia. They're still there. They're probably staring at us through the window. Let's wave at them, in case they're looking."

We both waved.

"I feel a right idiot," said Mike. "I bet they're not even looking. Are you getting the bus?"

"Yes, I am. Are you on your way to the shops? Aren't they all closed by now?"

"Just going to get a take-away from the place round the corner. For our supper. But I'll wait till the bus comes."

"It's OK, honestly. You don't have to . . ." I couldn't think of anything to say. I turned away a little just in case I was blushing. My face was certainly feeling a bit warm. We waited and waited, not saying anything much, although every now and then I could bear the silence no longer and began chattering about anything—Roland, Tricia, the play—until the bus finally came.

"See you tomorrow," I called out as I got on.

"Yes." He smiled and waved at me.

I could see him still standing at the bus stop for a long time. It was a straight road, and there he was, his outline getting tinier and tinier as the bus drove away. Then we turned the corner and I could no longer see even the speck that he'd become.

After supper, at about six-thirty, I telephoned the theater. George answered.

"Hello, George," I said. "It's Mel here . . . George, could I have a word with Chris, please? He's having an extra rehearsal. Really? No, I'm sure I heard he was having a late rehearsal tonight . . . no one at all? Oh, well don't worry, I'll see him in the morning. It's not important . . . Right, cheerio, George."

I put the phone down. No one had been in the theater at all since we'd left it around five o'clock. George knew nothing about extra rehearsals. Cheerio, George.

I sighed. Dinah and Chris had clearly decided not to put the stage staff out in any way, and had moved their rehearsal somewhere else. To Chris's flat perhaps? I waited till ten-thirty and then I telephoned Dinah, quite ready to have the whole matter out with her over the phone if I had to. Mummy Mouse answered.

I said: "Hello, this is Mel. Could I speak to Dinah, please."

Mummy Mouse said: "Oh, is that you, dear? No, well, Dinah isn't back yet . . . she rang up about half an hour ago and told us not to wait up. She said they'd had a bit of a late rehearsal at the theater and then she'd been to Tricia's house for a meal and not to worry. Tricia's dad would give her a lift home. I was just going to bed myself, actually."

"I'm sorry to ring so late."

Mummy Mouse said: "That's all right, dear. Shall I tell her you called?"

I said: "No, don't worry, I'll see her tomorrow morning at rehearsal. Good night."

I put the phone down and went to my bedroom. Tricia, I knew, had been going to the cinema with Roland tonight. Clare was in London. The Project was empty. Chris and Dinah were in Chris's flat and Stanislavsky himself didn't keep on with improvements and interpretations of the text until ten-thirty at night. I felt quite sure that Chris and Dinah were lovers by now, and that Clare, if she had ever been that close to Chris, was on her way out. I would tackle Dinah about it first thing, I decided. The last thought I had before I went to sleep was to wonder whether perhaps Clare knew already and whether that was the real reason for the trip to London . . . then I decided that she'd seemed too normal before she left. She couldn't possibly know, but then again I didn't know her well enough to predict how she would react. Maybe she was the bottle-it-all-up-and-don't-let-a-thing-show type. And maybe not.

That night I dreamed that I was running after Clare, following her from the Green Room, along the corridor and onto the stage, but when I caught up with her, she turned to look at me, and it was Dinah all the time, or maybe Clare with Dinah's face, I wasn't sure. The stage had vanished and we were in a bedroom where the sheets of the bed dipped and swirled like frosting on a cake, and paper doilies hung like curtains at the window.

I've said I'm not afraid of anything much, but I was a little apprehensive about seeing Dinah on Friday morning, mainly because I wasn't quite sure what I was going to say or what tone I was going to adopt. In many ways, the whole thing was (joke!) no affair of mine.

To begin with, I couldn't find her. She wasn't on stage or in the Green Room, she wasn't in the rest room or anywhere in the wings. I found her in one of the dressing rooms in the end, just sitting in front of one of the mirrors. As I came in, she said:

"Don't you just love these mirrors? I do. I've wanted one ever since I was little. One like this with light bulbs all around. I wonder if I can get my dad to put the bulbs up for me . . . but it wouldn't be the same . . . not with the kind of dressing table I've got, would it?"

"Dinah," I said, "I've got to ask you something."

"Well, don't look so serious, for God's sake, Mel. Spit it out."

I couldn't spit it out. Instead I mumbled and muttered so indistinctly that Dinah said:

"Whatever are you trying to say?"

"I'm asking . . . are you and Chris . . ." I couldn't bring my mouth to say the words aloud. "Are you . . . well . . . going together?"

Dinah looked into the mirror and made a kissing face. Then she smiled at me.

"Come on, Mel, it's not like you to be mealymouthed. I'll say it for you, since you're so shy. I expect it's just that you're so young. Yes, is the answer. We are lovers. Technically, ever since last night. Really, ever since the minute we set eyes on one another."

"Oh," I said. " 'Some Enchanted Evening' stuff, is it? Instant love? Just add boiling water and stir . . ."

"It does occur," said Dinah with dignity. "You may find out when you're older."

"It was just on your part, the fairy tale, wasn't it? Go on, admit it," I said. "I saw the way you were fluttering and leaning and looking and batting the old eyelashes till they nearly dropped off with the effort . . .'Oh, Chris, I don't understand what Irina's feeling here,' and 'Oh, Chris, why do I have to sit like this when I'd be more comfortable like this' . . . I've watched you waggling your legs about in those flimsy little frocks. I've been watching you. You can't fool me. You've made a dead set at him. He was perfectly happy with Clare until you came along. I saw them together even before you turned up at the audition . . . he loved her . . . and then you . . ." I was lost for words. In the end I said: "You turned his head. You . . . paraded yourself to such an extent that he didn't know whether he was coming or going."

Dinah, still looking into the mirror, let a deeply satisfied smile cross her face. Then she turned to me.

"You think I'm going to deny it, don't you? You think I'm going to say I couldn't help it, and I'm sorry and I would never hurt Clare in a million years and all that sort of shit, don't you? You think I'm going to be good little Dinah, isn't that right? Well, you're wrong. I'm not. Just listen to me. All my life I've grown up in that grotty little shop and it's not where I intend to stay any longer than I can help. It's just like Irina says: life *hasn't* been beautiful up till now . . . it bloody well nearly has choked me like a weed, but I'm getting out. I'm going to be famous, and I'll tell you another thing, I don't give a tuppenny damn who it is I have to step over to crawl out of the life I've had till now. I saw Chris that first day, and I knew. I knew at once that if only I could be in *this* show, get *this* part, then . . . well, anything was possible. And I was right."

"What do you mean?"

"He's given me a part in the next Project production." She laughed, I supposed, because my mouth had dropped open in amazement.

"Yes, darling, when all you sweet little kiddies have gone back to your dinky little schools, Borstals, or wherever, I shall be on the professional stage. I shall have an Equity card. I'm doing Desdemona."

I suppressed a desire to make a remark about hoping someone really *did* strangle her and said instead:

"There's seventy-five percent unemployment among Equity cardholders."

"I," she answered sweetly, "will be in the other twenty-five percent. Don't worry about me."

"Dinah, I'm not worried about you," I said. "What about Clare?"

"What about her?"

"Is Chris going to tell her? He must. He can't let her find out from a careless bit of backstage gossip. She'll be back tonight."

"Oh, he'll tell her. I don't think he wants to, mind, but I shall make him. I don't want any . . . misunderstandings. After all, she'll have to get over it in time to design *Othello*."

I couldn't believe it. "You mean Chris will want her to design his next show?"

"Yes, of course, why not? She's brilliant. Don't you think, Mel, you're being a bit—excuse the pun—melodramatic? Gosh, that's quite witty. I mean, Clare is a grown woman, divorced even. I'm sure she'll cope admirably. She seems quite self-contained to me."

I was furious by this time. I shouted:

"Just because she doesn't lick her glossy pink lips and wear no bra to rehearsal doesn't mean she has no feelings!"

Dinah shouted straight back:

"Is that so? Well, let me tell you direct from the horse's mouth, mind you, that she bloody well hasn't. She's a cold fish, get it? A cold fish!"

I wasn't finished with Dinah yet. I leaned right over her where she was sitting on the dressing table stool and hissed at her:

"That," I said, "is all you know. In your book, and Chris's book too, it seems, a cold fish is someone who shows a certain reticence about falling on her back the minute a bloke looks at her. Well, it's not. I've got quite another definition of a cold fish and it's this: someone who uses people for her own ends, someone who'll pretend she's in love just to play Desdemona and get an Equity card."

I turned to leave.

Dinah shouted after me: "It's not true! It isn't! What do you know about love anyway? I *do* love Chris. I do . . .

86

really I do . . ." She burst into tears. I came back into the room.

"Stop crying," I said. "Your mascara'll run and the rehearsal's in five minutes. Just give Chris the message, or I will. He's to tell Clare as soon as possible and in the nicest way he can. OK?"

Dinah sniffed.

"I suppose so. And Mel?"

"Yes?"

"Are we still friends? Can we be?"

"I don't feel very friendly at the moment, Dinah, and that's the truth. I might feel differently when I know she's OK—Clare, I mean."

"Mel, you can't help it, honestly you can't. Falling in love, I mean."

"That," I said, "is a load of unadulterated baloney. Sliced. On rye. With mustard." I left before she could say another word.

There was nothing I felt less like doing, after my scene with Dinah, than going and rehearsing, but I went. At least I had the satisfaction of knowing that it was Act Four we were doing, where Natasha comes into her own, and is beastly in the nicest possible way to the sisters: *"Irina,"* I said, *"you're leaving tomorrow and it's such a shame. Stay a few more days anyway, why don't you?"* Meaning, of course: I can't wait for you to leave and then I'll change your room around and cut down the avenue of firs and this whole place will be exactly as I want it.

Gradually, as Chris took us through the small scenes that make up the last act, I calmed down a little. From my position in the wings I watched them all, pretending to feelings that were not their own, taking on other people's gestures, actions, emotions, and I wondered (not for the

87

first time) if actors were ever to be trusted. Could they not act out parts in their private life as well, if it suited them to do so? Did you ever know where you were with an actor? If they professed love or friendship or sincerity, were you supposed to believe them? If they had twenty masks at their disposal, how were you to pick out one real face? Even Dinah had played the part of a soft, gentle, friendly, and charming person, and as far as I knew, everyone in the company was convinced and liked her—and why not? I had seen the real Dinah, the scheming, calculating, stop-at-nothing Dinah, or so I thought, but was that only another mask? Perhaps she was really just a little mouse-creature, like her mother, and had deliberately covered up her softness and anxiety and basic shyness with a shiny crust of ambition. I no longer knew. I didn't really care.

On stage, Louise was saying:

"We shall remain behind, on our own, to start our life again . . . We have to live . . ."

I thought: that's the point, of course. Everyone has to live, and in order to get through life every one of us puts on bits and pieces of disguise. We hide this or that from other people, hide all kinds of stuff from ourselves, don't admit the truth always, put on clothes, makeup, jewels, voices to create for ourselves a person we'll be able to bear looking at in the mirror every day, so I suppose we shouldn't go blaming actors for their chameleon-like qualities. Still, having said that, Dinah's performance as Irina was extraordinary. Everyone could see she was pure, innocent, noble, well meaning, and above all, honest. Candor blazed out of her eyes. I felt as if I could burst with rage at her duplicity.

"You've got to hand it to her," Mike said, coming up behind me in the wings. "She's bloody good."

"Yes," I said. "I wish I could like her better and admire her less."

"Did you talk to her?"

I nodded.

"Is it true?"

I nodded again.

Mike put his hand on my shoulder. "Come to the workshop tonight. We're painting flats for Act Four. It's very soothing work, painting, and Pete needs all the help he can get."

"Yes," I said, "thanks. I'd like that."

"About seven, then, OK?"

"OK."

The workshop was a huge cavern of a room that stretched almost the entire length of the theater, deep under the auditorium and the stage. It was full of wonderful smells: glue and paint and size and sawdust and the raw, pinkish smell of wooden planks, old velvet, new hessian, and a special kind of thick airlessness common to all underground spaces. It was cool and every sound reverberated around it. People walking on stage above our heads made footsteps like distant giants. Naked lightbulbs hung down from twisted flex and the light made shadows like black felt cutouts around every object. The props corner had beds in it with brass bedsteads, a silver samovar, potted plants, vases, a table, chairs, a trunk, a chest of drawers, fans, candlesticks, lamps, trinket boxes, bunches of paper flowers . . . I loved looking at it, seeing everything that appeared so real and grand and solid on the stage reduced to paint and papier-mâché and flimsiness down here. Pete, the chief carpenter and props man, the man in charge of making all the scenery, was small and bearded and quiet, like a cuddly troll. Janet, the Stage Manager, used to bring her sand-wiches and cups of tea down here whenever she could. We all assumed that she and Pete had a pleasant and comfortable relationship among the painted flats and snaky coils of rope that lurked in the corners. Pete also had two helpers, Gill and Keith, who came in to paint and make props and who, later on, would change the sets during the course of the play.

Mike was already there when I arrived, painting huge, pale green swishes onto an enormous flat, showing the avenue of firs disappearing into the distance.

"Grab a brush," he said.

"What am I supposed to do then?"

"Sky, I think . . . over there. Can you reach?"

"Yes, that's fine. Where's Pete?"

"He and Janet just went to get a bite at the Capricorn. They'll be back soon. Have you eaten?"

"Yes. What about you?" I'd looked on this painting business as a chance to get to know Mike a little better, a chance to find out more about him. Perhaps he would be more forthcoming now that we were alone. I hoped so. I hoped I wouldn't have to keep probing and enquiring.

"Yeah," he said, and went on painting in silence, seemingly absorbed and fascinated by the shiny green surface of a fir tree. So much for intimate revelations. A more drastic approach was definitely called for.

"Mike," I said, "why is it that you're so cagey? What are you hiding? Are you hiding something? Are you hiding it from everyone or just from me? Attempt all questions. Do not write on both sides of the paper at once."

He laughed. "I'm not actually hiding anything."

"Oh, no, not half! Full revelations every Sunday in the *News of the World*. Don't be silly. No one even knows where you live."

"I live in a terraced house about three hundred yards down the road. Don't look now, but here comes a flying address—ready? 35 Dukinfield Road," Mike said, and fell silent again.

"Wow," I said, "is that it?"

"What else do you want to know?"

"Everything."

"Everything . . ." Mike dipped his brush into the paint and thought about this for a few moments. "OK then, I guess I'll have to tell you now. It's not that I'm hiding anything really, you understand, it's just that life's a bit easier if you don't have to keep explaining all your problems to everyone."

"I'm not everyone, though, am I?"

"I know. That's why I'll tell you."

"I won't tell a soul, I promise."

"I don't mind," Mike said. "It's nothing to be ashamed of. It's only that I don't want to have to keep talking about it all the time."

"I won't tell anyone," I whispered.

Mike put his brush down on top of the tin of paint and turned to look at me.

"I live with my mother," he said. "She's divorced from my dad. There's only me. She's quite old . . . fifty-six . . . she had me very late, you see, and . . ." Mike paused. "Have you heard of agoraphobia?"

"Where you're frightened of open spaces?"

"That's right . . . well, she's got it, but it's not just open spaces, it's going out . . . anywhere. She hasn't left the house for three years . . . and . . . well, that's it really. I have to do the shopping or anything that needs doing outside the house."

I couldn't think of anything to say. Then:

"Won't she be able to come and see you in the play?"

"I don't know." Mike picked up his brush again. "She wants to, I know. She keeps talking and talking about it and she's better than she was. Some days she can go a little way down the garden path by herself, and if I'm with her, she can just about manage to cross the road to get some cigarettes, but only if I'm with her. I have to hold her hand all the time."

"Hasn't she got any friends who can help her?"

"Oh, yes, there's a couple of people . . . but that's another thing. She doesn't speak English all that well, and she's dead ashamed of the way she speaks with a thick foreign accent and that makes her scared to meet new people. She's got her own little circle of friends who all speak Polish, and she always has had, ever since she came here, and that was during the War. Well . . . you can see why I don't spread all the details of my life around."

"Can I visit you?" I said, painting blue sky as hard as I could with my back to Mike because I didn't want to see his answer before I heard it. "I'd like to meet your mother. I bet you haven't told her how good you are as Vershinin."

Mike laughed. "We talk of little else. Actually, she's a big Chekhov fan. She even reads it in Russian." He frowned. "She'd love to come and see it."

"My mother could fetch her in the car. She'd look after her. Really. Can I meet your mother? Can I speak to her? Maybe together we could persuade her."

"I wouldn't count on it," Mike said, "but of course you can meet her. She likes my friends coming to the house, but not many of them do. It's hard work and people are always so busy."

"I'd love to come. I'll come whenever you say I can." I'd stopped painting for the last few moments, but something in Mike's face made me turn away from him and dip my brush into the pot of sky-blue liquid at my feet.

"Mel," he asked softly, and the way he said it made me feel fluttery in the stomach quite suddenly and I could hear my own heartbeats very loud in a part of my head. "Put your brush down, I don't want pale blue paint all over everything." He leaned forward and took the brush from my hand and placed it very gently on top of the paint pot. And then he kissed me. My stomach felt as though I were on a roller coaster lurching away on a crazy journey of its own. I closed my eyes tight, and all at once it was lovely, and the things I'd worried about and dreaded (like where do the noses go and what happens to your breathing and how long is it meant to go on for) simply fell away and I felt a giant wave of pure elation wash over me, as if I'd suddenly discovered I could swing through the air on a flying trapeze, or knew how to swallow dive from the highest board of all, cleaving the turquoise satin surface of the water like a blade.

"Mel," Mike said, and I couldn't think of a word to utter, so I just said:

"Mike," and we both burst out laughing.

"I don't know what to say next," he said.

"Nor me. This is obviously why all love scenes are conducted in sighs and moans and oohs and aahs. No one can think of anything sensible to say."

"Let me kiss you again and then we won't need to say anything for a bit."

"But what about this flat? It'll never get painted at this rate."

"Who cares?"

We didn't, until some fake coughing told us that Pete and Janet had returned from the Capricorn.

"Sorry to break it up and everything," Pete was grinning from ear to ear, "but there's work to be done."

We painted our pieces of sky and fir tree. We talked

quietly and giggled at things that weren't funny at all. Dinah and Chris and Clare—everyone else and all their problems seemed, for a time, to be very far away at the end of a dark tunnel. Every time I looked at Mike, I felt as if I were holding the whole of myself close to a source of light and warmth. Every thought in my head was blossoming out, I felt, like a tiny flower and I had the distinct impression that the blood was fizzing along through my veins like sparkling wine.

By nine o'clock, my arm felt as if it were about to part company with my body. Mike said:

"We'll fix a time for you to come round."

I nodded.

"Mel?"

"Yes?"

"Thanks."

"What for?"

"I don't know . . . I'll see you, Mel."

"Yes."

"Good night."

"See you tomorrow."

He blew me a kiss as he left. I washed my hands in the sink in the corner and said good-bye to Pete and Janet. On my way home I noticed that the ancient clichés about walking on air, the pavement always staying beneath my feet before, etc., and so forth, were all perfectly true. I wondered if this was being properly in love, and if anyone could see it on my face. It had all happened rather quickly. Perhaps Dinah was right and it *did* just strike you like lightning. There you are, walking quietly along a kind of metaphorical cliff-path, liking someone a lot, when just one kiss can send you hurtling over the edge, into Love, which is like a vast warm sea waiting to engulf you. Would my mother notice that I was somehow different? What would they say at rehearsal? Would Mike still feel the same tomorrow? Would I?

My mother had left a note on the kitchen table: "Gone to the movies with Lily. Back about eleven. Lots of things in fridge. Love, M." I wondered: would my face, transfigured and made radiant by love, last the night? Or would I be back to normal by the morning? I had a slice of cold pizza and some apple juice and thought about Mike's mother, frightened to leave her house. What sort of a house was it? I imagined it for some reason being very bare, with wide spaces between the pieces of furniture, like my uncared-for dolls' house in the attic, with Mike and his mother small figures moving from one near-empty room to another, walking on drab carpets, looking at the empty walls.

Mike comes to see me almost every day. Sometimes I imagine him to be a boatman rowing between my island and the island his mother lives on permanently. He visits the mainland (school, the outside world) from time to time, but really, his life is spent rowing between us. His mother's island I picture as volcanic and storm-tossed, thick with vines and creepers and growing things. It has rocky coves and great white cliffs all around it and sea birds cry as they wheel in the sky above it. My island, on the other hand, is straight out of Gauguin, with talcum-powder sand and purple hills and luscious fruits growing from plants swelling and green with life. I am, I realize, not being entirely fair to Mike's mother, whom I like and for whom I feel sorry at all times when I'm not busy being sorry for myself all alone and bored to death on my sickbed. I have been better, though, since Clare presented me with the ice-cream book, but looking back on what I've just written, I see that the night we painted the scenery down in Pete's basement was the night before everything: the night before Chris told Clare, the night before I met Mike's mother, and the night before we tried *Three Sisters* out for the first time without books. That was on Saturday morning.

That same morning the sun was shining as I reached the theater. That's something I remember particularly because there was so little warmth and light from the weather this past summer that any day on which the sky was blue, any day on which you could leave your coat in the Green Room as you walked to the Capricorn for lunch, was memorable. It was also on this day that I noticed neat parcels of gray and red bricks, all square and held together with metal ribbons, dotted about on the wasteground. The hillocks of earth had grown too, into quite high piles, small mountains of soft brown powdery sand growing beside large holes. It had begun to look as though someone was digging the foundations of a building. I found the sight of all those clean new bricks very encouraging. Together with the sunshine on that Saturday morning, I took them for a good omen, and a symbol of things growing, developing, coming into fruition. So elated was I at these signs of life and hope that I forgot to be nervous about doing without the books, right up to the time I took my seat with the others in the auditorium.

Chris did his best to make us feel at ease. "I don't want you to worry in the slightest, any of you. Janet is in the Prompt corner, and why it's called the Prompt Corner is because she's ready to prompt, and you are all, without exception, going to make thousands of mistakes. YOU ARE TO SOLDIER ON AND NOT WORRY. OK?"

We all nodded and said, yes, we'd be fine, and then we

took up our positions for Act One and began to stumble through the play.

It was like jumping into the sea without a life jacket, like crossing the high wire without a safety net, like the seconds between jumping out of an airplane and your parachute opening extended into minutes at a time. It was bloody terrifying. We all groaned and muttered and swore and the sounds that were heard above all the rest were Chris's cheerful: "Go on, you're doing fine . . . go on . . . just get through it . . ." and Janet's monotonous prompts from downstage right. By lunchtime, as Charlie so picturesquely put it, our nerves were "hanging out all over the place like snapped piano strings." Everyone on stage was completely convinced that we would never in a million years have a play ready for performance in three weeks' time.

"You will all be word perfect," Chris assured us. "I promise you. I know."

Who did he think he was kidding? The whole thing would be a disaster from beginning to end.

"OK, break for lunch," Chris said. "That was very good, considering." (Hollow laughter from all sides) "We'll start again at two-thirty sharp, and do it all over again, and you'll see, it'll be better."

Everyone drifted away. Lunch arrangements hovered in the air like birds:

"Coming to the Capricorn?"

"Yeah."

"Me too. Wait for me."

"I'm staying in the Green Room. I can't go on this afternoon without looking through the play again."

"I'll stay with you. I've got sandwiches."

"I haven't."

"Charlie, bring us back a sandwich."

"Right."

"Get me one, too, then, OK?"

"Give us the money then."

"Has anyone got change for the coffee machine?"

Mike said: "Will you be OK if I dash home for a bit? I mean, you could come, too, if you like, but I'd rather you came when there's more time."

"That's all right. I've also got a lot to look at. I'm staying right here."

"See you then." He smiled and touched my cheek with the tips of his fingers. I took this to mean he had no regrets about the previous evening, and I made my way happily to the Green Room, ready to work hard at the play before two-thirty.

Dinah was curled up on the sofa that best set off her ivory complexion: a battered old number upholstered in what must once have been royal blue velvet. I very pointedly said nothing, and sat down as far away from her as I possibly could, but she wasn't having any of that, and got up and came to sit right beside me.

"Still cross with me?"

I sniffed in a manner I hoped was haughty. "I wouldn't have thought it would bother you either way."

"I just think all our performances suffer, if we can't pull together as a company in a friendly sort of way."

"That's Chris talking, not you," I said. "And may I ask where old Lover Boy is this lunchtime?"

"You should know."

"Should I?"

"Yes. You suggested it. He's taken Clare to the pub, hasn't he? To break the news."

I said nothing. My sandwich began to taste like cardboard.

99

I opened my copy of the play to go over the scene where Natasha, on the night of the fire, tells Olga that the nanny, Anfisa, must go. She's horribly rude. She says:

"And I want that thieving old bag out of the house by tomorrow . . . that old witch! How dare people cross me so, how dare they?" Poor old Anfisa, the girls' old nanny! Dismissed. Sent packing. Natasha is ruthless in organizing things just the way she wants them. She looks at everything and considers how it will affect her. Even the fire that burns down Kirsanov Lane is used to show what good sleepers her two children are: *"Bobik and Sofochka are fast asleep for all the world as if nothing had happened."* I looked at Dinah and thought what a wonderful Natasha she would make. Look at her, I thought, delicately biting into her sandwich with mouse-sharp teeth, knowing that somewhere quite nearby, Clare was . . . what was Clare doing? I could not imagine what Chris would say . . . what she would say . . . would she come back to the theater after lunch? All her bits and pieces of paper and material were still on one of the seats in the auditorium. I decided to keep an eye out for her, and at two-fifteen I went to stand as unobtrusively as possible in the passage leading from the Stage Door to the Green Room. Everyone had to come in that way. At two-twenty, Mike arrived. He grinned when he saw me.

"Are you waiting for me?"

I couldn't grin back. I felt slightly sick. I shook my head and told him why I was there.

"Chris has a key to the front of the house, you know. I've just seen him and Clare going in that way."

"Oh, crikey . . . and I can't go and look for her now . . . we're starting in five minutes."

"Come into the auditorium, then. They've got to come in there eventually."

"Right."

Janet's voice came over the tannoy.

"Act One beginners, on stage please. Beginners on stage. Everyone else into the auditorium."

We waited until two forty-five for Chris to appear. Everybody was whispering and wondering and most people had a good idea where he was. I wasn't the only person who had commented about Dinah. In that quarter of an hour, I realized that what Chris had told us on the first day was perfectly true: we knew one another so well that it was quite hopeless trying to keep anything secret. So much of us was exposed by the simple fact of walking on-to a stage displaying our emotions that we could pick up signals from one another as if by a kind of telepathy. This morning, for example, Mike and I had been standing in the wings not even speaking to one another, when Charlie appeared behind us, put one arm around each of us, and drew us into a tight hug, with his clown's face sandwiched between our two heads.

"Like that, is it, me darlings?" he said in a fake Irish accent.

"Like what?" Mike laughed.

"Like love, baby" (switch to American). "Stands out a mile. Can't fool your uncle Charlie. Besides, everybody knows about everybody around here."

It was quite true. We all knew everything. Who had lunch with/sat with/went home with/shared a copy of the play with whom, and also, of course, when they ceased to do all those things.

When Chris walked into the back of the auditorium that day, Louise, who was sitting behind me, whispered:

"Uh oh . . . Trouble. Watch yourselves."

She was quite right. We all stiffened in our seats and fell silent. Chris looked around, searching for Dinah. I looked at her. She was smiling at him, raising her eyebrows a little. Questioning. He gave a nod which he hoped would be imperceptible to anyone except Dinah, but I saw it, and probably everyone else did, too.

"OK, people, I'm very sorry I'm late. Let's get going, shall we, and see how well we can manage this time."

We began the play, drifting about among the words and sentences like little paper boats bobbing along on the surface of a fast-flowing stream. At the beginning of Act One, I knew it was a good fifteen or twenty minutes before my first entrance. I decided I could bear the suspense no longer—I would go and look for Clare. She wasn't in the Green Room, which was the first place I looked, nor in the loo, which is a good place in which to cry on your own. I was just wondering whether I could risk going up to wardrobe to see if she was there, when I suddenly remembered her car. I ran to the Stage Door and looked into the car park. Clare's car had gone. George was sitting in his cubbyhole looking morose behind a copy of the *Daily Mirror*.

"George," I said, "have you seen Clare?"

George nodded. "She's been clattering my dustbins something awful," he said. "I'd just opened the door to ask her to be a bit quieter when I saw her driving off on a cloud of dust in that funny car of hers."

"Why would she be rattling the bins?" I asked.

George looked at me pityingly.

"Well, why would anyone rattle the bins? Go on, ask yourself. 'Cos they're throwing something away, right? She must have been getting rid of some rubbish or something."

"Thanks, George." I looked at my watch. Listened to Louise saying to Mike:

"You were a lieutenant then and you were in love with

somebody and why it was I don't know, but everyone used to tease you by calling you the major ..."

I was quite safe. Still another ten pages or so before my entrance. I slipped out of the Stage Door and opened the first of George's squeaky-clean dustbins. What I saw inside made me feel so ill that I sat down on the back steps of the theater and put my head between my legs. Clare's model of the set, the four little rooms with their miniature furnishings, had been carefully and deliberately broken into very small pieces indeed. Little scraps of curtain had been torn from the windows, doll-sized chairs and tables had been crushed and splintered, the framework had been stood on and trampled and the screen made from lace doilies had evidently been squeezed in a fist and snapped in half. A giant had taken the Prozorovs' house and destroyed it. The anger behind this destruction terrified me. Clare could do anything, if she was in this state. I knew at once that someone had to find her ... reach her and talk to her ... and I knew exactly what I had to do. I ran back into the theater and burst on to the stage, just as Andrew was singing the praises of work:

"I worked from first thing in the morning until eleven at night ..."

"Stop it!" I shouted. "Chris, stop this rehearsal!"

A silence fell. Chris said:

"Mel, have you taken leave of your senses? What are you doing, interrupting us like this? There'd better be a bloody good reason for it, like a fire or something."

"There is," I yelled. "While you've been having play-play feelings down here, all frightfully solemn and meaningful, someone has been really hurt. It's Clare. She's gone. Her car's not there and she's taken the model of the set and broken it into a thousand pieces and stuffed them all

103

into George's dustbin—and I think someone should go after her and see she's all right, that's all." I burst into tears and sat down on the chaise lounge. While the silence around grew deeper, I felt Mike's hand stroking my hair. After what seemed like a very long moment, Chris spoke:

"OK, everyone. I'm sorry about this. I suppose I owe you all an explanation. The thing is, Clare will no longer be working on this show. She and I have . . . well, we've split up. I told her today and she decided that she was going down to London for a while to stay with her family. It's been a hard time for all of us . . ." (Oh, you crumb-bum, I thought. What's been hard about it for you? Or for Dinah, come to that? Haven't you both got exactly what you've wanted all along?) . . . "but I'm sure," Chris continued, "if we all pull together and work hard, we'll be able to manage all right. I was going to ask if any of you knew of anyone who could give a hand in the costume department."

Revenge, how blissfully sweet you are sometimes! Oh, Dinah, how I enjoyed saying what I said next and seeing the look on your face!

"Mrs. McLaren, Dinah's mother," I said, "is a dab hand with a needle and what's more, very keen indeed to be a part of this show."

Chris smiled at Dinah, who had to change her expression from sour to sweet in the twinkling of an eye. Seeing the way she did it was a lesson in acting I'll never forget.

"Is that right, Dinah?" Chris said. "Would your mother be willing to help?"

"Oh, yes," Dinah said, silky as silky can be. "She'd love it. I'll tell her to come and see Ruby, shall I?"

"Great," Chris said. "Now can we all get on, please? We've lost a lot of time today. Start from *'Lunch is served . . . we're having a pie.'*"

And that was Clare, as far as Chris and the production were concerned. As I moved to my place in the wings I could hardly see for a mist of rage that clouded my eyes. Cliché Number Three of the theater, I thought. The show must go on. People breaking their hearts, falling sick, being miserable, being angry, leaving: all frightfully tough luck, of course, but the show must go on . . . well, why the hell must it? Who says it must? And who says that you can't take a short rest now and then to allow real life to break through for a bit? Would it have killed Chris to take the afternoon off and talk to Clare for a little longer? No, of course it wouldn't, but he's a busy little spider, isn't he, busy running around connecting threads into a web of fantasy emotions felt by fictional characters . . . I thought his behavior was dreadful. Dinah passed me in the wings at the end of Act One.

"Thank you very much," she hissed between clenched teeth, her eyes like glass. "Just what I'd always wanted, my bloody mother working on the show."

"Serves you right," I hissed back. "I hope she takes up permanent residence in your dressing room from now till the end of the last performance."

I went down into the auditorium to collect Clare's things from the chair in the third row where she'd been sitting. Chris didn't even care enough about her to see that her things were safe, I thought, as I gathered them together.

"Mel?" It was Chris. I didn't feel like talking to him just then.

"What do you want?"

"Well, to explain, really. I couldn't in front of everyone. Mel, just sit down and look at me, can't you? I want to tell you something . . . I want you to know . . . that I feel really terrible about Clare. Really guilty, I mean, I liked her so much."

"You loved her till Dinah came along. I saw you."

"Well, maybe. Or I thought I did. Till I met Dinah. I mean, I didn't want to hurt Clare . . . and quite honestly, I didn't know she'd be this angry and this upset. But Mel, these things happen and you can't help it. Sometimes people can't help falling in love."

"I'm not one hundred percent convinced of that. I think in lots of cases, people go around looking for a kind of puddle of love to fall into, and when they see something that looks likely, they plunge in regardless."

"Mel, you're so young. You're not even seventeen . . ."

"And Dinah, I suppose, is middle-aged, is she?"

"She's eighteen. It makes a difference."

"Evidently. Anyway, you don't have to apologize to me."

"You're Clare's friend. I can see you care more than anyone else."

"It's lucky someone does, isn't it? Lucky that I've even begun to get her things together to take to her flat. That'll save you lots of trouble, won't it?"

"Yes, it will, and thank you, Mel. You shouldn't be so hard on me. I haven't been dishonest with Clare, have I? I've told her the truth."

"So that's OK then? All's fair in love and war . . . is that it?"

"To some extent, yes, that's true. Look at the play. Look at the three sisters. Who does your heart ache for in the last act? It's Masha and Vershinin, not poor old Kulygin, the cuckold, the unfortunate husband."

"Speak for yourself," I muttered, picking up the last bits of paper from under Clare's seat. "I for one am on Kulygin's side, so there!"

I made my way to the Green Room thinking: I must simmer down a bit before I go home. I had visions of a pensive half hour with Olly, stroking him absentmindedly while I brooded on the fickleness of human emotion. Unfortunately, Louise and Matt were already there, sitting rather close together on the blue sofa, which had a tendency to roll its occupants into a deep central crater. They sprang apart as I came in.

"Don't mind me," I said, "I'm in such a state I'm not really noticing anything around me."

"You won't say a word though, Mel, will you?" Louise whispered. "To Andrew. Or to anyone else really. Will you?"

"Have you given Andrew the push?" I said.

"No," Matt said. "I'm trying to persuade her, but it's hard work. And I've got to go home now. Will I see you later on, Louise?"

Louise sniffed. I noticed then that her eyes were red. I wondered what I'd interrupted, why she'd been crying.

"I'll phone you, Matt," she said. "Honest I will."

"Right. 'Bye then," and Matt was gone.

I sat down next to Louise. "What's this then?" I said. "Chris has just broken up with Clare and gone off with Dinah, and now it's you and Andrew."

"I don't know what to do." Louise wiped the corner of one eye with the back of her hand. "I mean, Matt likes me and I fancy him, but I don't know if I like him as much as I like Andrew and anyway I'd feel mean if I dropped Andrew now, so close to the performance. I don't know what to do. Tell me what to do, Mel."

"I can't tell you . . . you've got to decide. But whatever you do decide you'll have to let Andrew know. There's no way you can keep this Matt business a secret. Not if you're constantly cuddling on sofas and springing apart when people come in."

"If only Andrew would *do* something . . . something exciting. I don't know."

"Kill a dragon? Did you have that sort of thing in mind?"

"No, don't be silly. I just mean, something unexpected . . . something weird. He's so ordinary, so conventional."

"And Matt isn't, I suppose? Honestly, Louise, you're a fool. Just because his jacket's got a few studs on it, and just because he's a better actor than Andrew, you've let your head get turned."

"You think I should stick to Andrew, don't you?"

"I'm not saying what I think. I don't think. Not really. It's just that if any more people get hurt around here, it's not going to be too much fun, is it?"

"I wouldn't tell him till after all this was over."

"Because it might spoil his performance?"

"Well, it very well might," said Louise. "To say nothing of my performance. As it is, I'm terrified half the time. I don't know all my words and I have nightmares practically every night about being out there and suddenly I haven't got a voice anymore. Truly, it's awful. I know all the words in this dream, and I'm mouthing them all, only no one can hear a sound . . . it's all silent. Everything I'm saying comes out silent. I'm dead scared."

"Don't worry," I said. "You're actually ever so good . . . and Masha's meant to be tense, edgy, and nervous for a lot of the time. It won't matter a bit if you're trembling like a leaf."

"Really? Do you really think so?"

"Oh, yes. And as for Andrew and Matt, I'd try and keep them firmly at the back of your mind till the play's over, and deal with that problem then."

"I suppose so." She sighed and picked up her coat from the arm of the sofa. "I wish life weren't so bloody complicated. Good night, Mel."

" 'Night, Louise," I shouted after her. "It'll sort itself

out." I don't know if I believed that, but it seemed a comforting thing to say.

Later that same evening, on my way home, I took Clare's things to her flat. Even though it was still quite light outside, there was a lamp burning in one of the downstairs rooms of Hansel and Gretel's cottage, dissolving the green twilight that filled it at every hour of the day.

"She's gone," Mrs. Sandler told me, empty-handed for once, not expecting anybody.

"Did she say when she'd be back?"

"No . . ." Mrs. Sandler shook her head. "She seemed a bit upset. Do you know what's the trouble?"

I didn't know what Clare would want me to say. I didn't know what Mrs. Sandler already knew. I said:

"I think she's overworked . . . she needs a bit of time off, I expect."

"Yes, yes, certainly she is overworked. Often she works late into the night."

"So could I just leave this stuff? And . . . have you got her address and phone number in London?"

"Somewhere . . ." Mrs. Sandler scrabbled through a pile of old, brown envelopes and shiny "Ten pence off" coupons on the hall table. "Yes, here it is."

I copied it carefully into my notebook. Later on, maybe tomorrow or the next day, I would ring Clare and speak to her, see how she was, assure her that we (or at least I) felt for her, and wanted to know she was all right.

My mother said:

"Clare came round this afternoon. She left a big brown envelope for you."

"Clare? Was she all right? What did she say? Oh, Mum, tell me every detail."

"Why, what's happened?"

"Honestly, Mum, it's such a long story . . ."

"I've got time . . . whatever's the good of having a daughter in a show if I can't get the benefit of all the good gossip?"

"It's not gossip. It's sad."

"Tell," said my mother, gathering her coffee cozily into her reach. "Tell all."

I told. My mother nodded at the end.

"It figures. She looked a bit washed out, I thought. Poor kid. Serves that Dinah right, having her mum there . . . but you know, I'd be happy to help as well, you know . . ."

"You might have to . . ." I looked down at the floor. "Have I told you about Mike?"

"I've heard the name. Here and there." (She was being dead casual. I could hear the effort she was putting into it.) "Is that a story, too?"

" 'Fraid so."

"Go on."

"Are you sure it won't keep?" I was shy of telling her about Mike, now that the moment had come.

"Get it off your chest, dear. You'll feel better . . ."

So again, I told. My mother did a good job trying to look even more nonchalant than before, but I could see she was pleased. Relieved. Like a young mum whose baby has been a bit late starting to walk, but who's managed it at last. She gave me a big hug and a kiss and went away to plaster nourishing unguents on her face and commune in private with my father's picture. I looked at the big, brown envelope Clare had left for me, frightened to open it.

"This is ridiculous," I said aloud in the empty kitchen, ripping it open at last. "It's not a letter bomb or anything." Clare had left me all the costume designs, fifteen of them, each one with a scrap of material stapled to it. There was also a note:

Dear Mel,

I'm going away for a couple of weeks—you'll understand why, I'm sure. It seems I was wrong about myself, about Chris, about everything. There you go.

Here are the designs. Ruby'll know how they should be made up (the ones that can't be cobbled together from old Laura Ashley blouses, etc.) and I've put a bit of the fabric on each one as kind of a guide. I'm very sorry to leave the show at this stage and I know you'll all have to be flying around trying to find people to do my work, but I can't help it.

Mel, please don't write or phone. I don't feel like talking to anyone at the moment. I'll be in touch when I get back.

Love,
Clare

September has come to an end and the weather on my tropical island is tropical. For the last couple of days, all the warmth and sunshine missing from the rest of the summer has been squeezing itself into the small space left between now and the beginning of autumn. Flies and wasps try buzzing, find they lack the energy, and end up mumbling in the corners of windows, up against the glass. The light is honey-beige; the air hangs thick from the trees and lies like veils around the streetlights in the evening. The heat itself has a quality of weariness about it, as if the summer were falling asleep: sighing quietly and closing its eyes.

But it is hot. The pen is slipping about in my fingers. My concession to the temperature is to lie on top of all the bedclothes and eat ice cream which I allow to melt so that I can swirl it around to resemble the covers of this book. Outside my window, I can see people walking about in summer clothes. Probably they've had to reopen trunks:

112

they'd put away their cottons for this year and, lo and behold, here's some more good weather so out they must all come again. I think of Mike's mother, who, as far as I know, doesn't own any clothes that are not woolly or tweedy. Poor thing. She must be gasping for breath.

The day Mike took me to see her was chilly, so the fact that she was wearing a hairy wool skirt and a jumper didn't strike me as unusual. But I've seen her many times since then and she's always, even on sunny days (and there were a couple), worn variations on this theme. Sometimes the jumper is fluffy and the skirt smooth, sometimes they're both fluffy, or both smooth, sometimes they're plain and sometimes they're patterned, but they have two constant features: they are always woolly and always in shades of pink: blush, sunset, coral, baby, dusky, shell, salmon—take your pick. On occasion they will blossom into browns, but even then, it's the pale beige-browns that look as if they're apologizing for being such a shameful thing as a color in the first place.

If Mrs. Corderly was pink, then the house was green. It was, of course, quite different from how I'd imagined it. There was too much furniture and not too little, and most of it was upholstered in khaki-green velvety fabric. I've never in my whole life seen so many plants in such a small space. It was as though Mrs. Corderly had tried, because she was unable to face the real outdoors, to bring a potted version of it into her house. There were ferns and rubber plants and small bushes lurking behind chairs and sofas and tables of cacti set up in front of every window and plants Mrs. Corderly told me were called succulents. The name suited them perfectly: they had plump, fleshy, velvety-looking leaves of grayish-green with a bloom to it, like skin.

"It takes a very long time," Mrs. Corderly said slowly

in her careful, foreign-sounding English, "to give them to drink. See, I have the special watering pot." She showed me a little plastic watering can with a long, thin spout, and I imagined her hovering over the plants with it, pictured it as a kind of extension of her thin body, as if she were a fluffy pink flamingo and the spout a kind of beak that she dipped into each green heart in turn.

She was pleasant, and polite and anxious that I should eat the small cakes that she had made for the occasion. If Mike had not told me about her disability, I would never have been able to guess. She seemed quite ordinary to me.

"But that's the whole point," Mike said later. "Nobody really takes the problem seriously, because the sufferer can seem so normal most of the time. I think a lot of people, those who don't know any better, think she brings it on herself. There's definitely a feeling of: why doesn't she pull her socks up and stop being so silly and just open the front door and go out, then?"

"I don't think that," I said. "I can see how awful it would be . . . to be imprisoned like that and not be able to do anything about it."

"She is trying," Mike said. "And you could see she was thinking very hard about what you said to her. Perhaps there is a slight chance that she'll be able to come . . . I doubt it, though."

We'd spoken a lot about *Three Sisters,* that first time. Mrs. Corderly seemed to know the whole play by heart. "I think," she said, "it is Chekhov knowing that all will change. He speaks of a great storm and in one year it is 1905 and in fifteen years it is the Russian Revolution. This he does not know, but in a way he does know. He knows that the old life is finished . . . the life of under the Czar. He can see, no? that this is not a way for the people to be living."

"Mike is going to be a very good Vershinin," I said. "You should come to the first night."

Her eyes widened. She looked, even at the mention of leaving the house, as if she'd like to burrow down behind the nearest sofa. Mike put his mug down on the floor, ready to say something soothing, but I went on:

"Mike has told me that it's hard for you to leave the house, but maybe if my mother came for you in the car and brought you straight back?"

"You are very kind," she nodded. "Everyone is kind. But for me it is so difficult. And for your mother it will be maybe difficult also. We see. We see later. I wish so much I could be at this play. For Michael and also for the play." She smiled at me. "You understand. I, too, am far from home."

I ate my little cake in silence, thinking of Mrs. Corderly as a young girl, fleeing her native Poland, coming to a country which would be home to her for the rest of her life, and yet not home. Perhaps she came from a landscape of birch trees, maples, and firs: forests and broad, rushing rivers. Perhaps she longs to return. It struck me then, all at once, how many people there must be who feel that they are in the wrong place, exiled, not where they should be. Either they look back and long to return like the three sisters, Mrs. Corderly, and even (to a certain extent) me, or else they're not happy with the place they are in and long to escape, like Dinah. It also occurred to me how important your feelings for other people are in this matter. Since rehearsing for *Three Sisters* and more particularly since meeting Mike, I had thought hardly at all about my grandmother's house, and not only that, the way I saw things was different. Even the muddy hillocks and lone cement mixers outside the theater had begun to look good to me, and I'd stopped mourning the demolition of old

115

houses and begun to wonder what shiny new buildings would go up in their place. There's nothing like a bit of love to make you feel you were in the right place at the right time, and doing all the right things—in other words, happy.

These philosophical musings flashed through my mind in the time it took to finish my cake. Mike had been talking about the set, telling his mother in detail what was in every scene. Mrs. Corderly smiled:

"I have upstairs a silver candelabra from my mother. With six arms for candles. It is from Russia, from long ago, perhaps from Chekhov's time, who knows? Will they use it, do you think?"

"We'll ask, Mother," Mike said. "I can take it in to show Chris."

"Tomorrow," said Mrs. Corderly. "Take it in tomorrow."

I said: "Then if it's used you'll have two reasons to come and see it. The play, I mean. Mike, and your candelabra."

She smiled. "Please God," she said, "I try."

Mike walked with me to the bus stop, talking all the way. Then he kissed me good-bye and we fell silent. I think both of us were uncomfortable about saying all the words that seem to go with the feelings: everything I wanted to tell him sounded so silly when I said it to myself. Love, I thought to myself on the bus going home that night, needs a totally new vocabulary. All the old words have been recited far too often by people in situations of extreme soppiness. Perhaps I wasn't really in love. Maybe you were only properly in love when all those words fell on your ears like sweet music and tumbled out of your mouth in a carefree and uninhibited fashion.

———

Slowly, painfully we grew used to doing without our little white, red-bordered texts. As we picked our way across the stage, from chalk mark to piece of furniture and back again, everyone became braver. Not having to hold a book in your hands frees you to do all sorts of things. It is at once easier to move in character. Roland seemed to get paunchier by the minute, and developed a stomach-smoothing, picking-crumbs-off-his-waistcoat gesture. Louise's hands were never still for very long and played, at moments of stress, with a lock of her hair. Chris seized on these movements, placed them where they would add to rather than take away from the words that were being spoken. All around us, the production was gathering momentum. The lighting designer, called Tim, shone different colored lights on to the stage, trying things out. Pete would emerge from time to time, from his underground lair to show Chris a plant pot or a cushion, and sometimes he would drag him off to the nether regions to inspect a piece of the set. Mrs. Corderly's candelabra became the centerpiece of the feast for Irina's name day. The avenue of firs flat, which Mike and I had helped to paint (OK, we hadn't exactly bust a gut over it) a few nights ago, was declared totally wrong. Much too dark, Chris said. "Like a wet weekend at Morecambe, for God's sake." Matt and Simon and Ruth volunteered to give Pete a hand at redoing it. And all of a sudden, we all became conscious of the fact that we were acting. A whole gang of us even discussed it, I remember, one lunchtime at the Capricorn. Mike and I were there, Charlie and Simon, Roland and Andrew and Louise, Tricia and even Dinah and Chris. Chris said:

"There are two kinds of actors, really. Whatever the director says or does to help them. There's the kind that become the part."

117

"That's me," said Simon. "Method acting. I feel, when I'm on stage, as if I *am* Tusenbach. I mean, if I wasn't . . . if I was aware of being Simon pretending to be Tusenbach, I'd run off the stage, terrified. Every time I go on, I have to think myself into *being* the Baron."

"But you can't," said Andrew. "Not really. There's always a bit of you that knows it's Simon, isn't there?"

"Oh, I suppose so," said Simon. "A bit. I think probably the smaller that bit is, the better you are as an actor."

"But not everyone's like that," Dinah said. "I mean I feel all the things Irina's supposed to feel, but I always know it's just me pretending, and I know, because I can see her, that Janet is in her corner and the audience is there. I mean, well, I never forget myself completely. Not to the extent of becoming Irina."

"That's the kind of acting where you use a lot of technique," said Tricia. "I'm like that. I mean, when I'm not in a scene, actually involved in it, I can be thinking of what I'd like for tea."

"Shame!" Chris smiled. "What an admission, Tricia. Still, you'll find it a bit different in performance."

"You haven't mentioned," Charlie said, "a third kind of acting."

"Is there one?"

"Of course. Only this one's only used by the really great stars."

"And what's it called, this method?" Chris grinned.

"It's being utterly yourself in every single role, so that you're more important than the part. *You're* what they come to see, like . . . well, John Wayne. He was always John Wayne. He was a star. Always the same."

"And someone like Dustin Hoffman is an actor: always different," Chris pondered. "Charlie might have a point."

118

"I'd rather be an actor any day," said Simon.

"Me, too," said Louise. "I'd like to be unrecognizable sometimes."

"Not me," said Dinah. "I'd like to be both a star and an actress. There are lots of those around, whatever you say, Charlie. Good actors and actresses who are some-how—I don't know—more than just that, like Glenda Jackson, or Vanessa Redgrave, or Meryl Streep. There are lots."

"So what makes a good actor?" I wanted to know. "Apart from this natural indefinable talent."

"Intelligence," said Mike.

"Lack of inhibition" (Andrew).

"Bravery," said Chris.

Louise asked, "Why bravery?"

"Well. . ." Chris thought for a moment. "It's tough. You expose yourself on a public stage. People can laugh at you, boo you, write horrible things about you in the paper, and above all you have to be prepared for hard work, very little money, and almost unavoidable years of unemployment."

"Then I reckon," Charlie said, "madness has to be a qualification for actors. You've got to be out of your skull to do it for a living."

"So why," Roland said, "are so many people just dying to get on to the stage, into TV or the movies? It can't be a desire to get rich. There have to be easier ways of doing that, surely."

"Acting," I said feebly, "acting is enjoyable. People en-joy it."

"But why?" Chris asked. "What is it about acting that's so enjoyable?"

That silenced everyone. Then Louise said:

"I like it because you get to know everyone so well. It's

119

like being in a team, or something like that. All in the same situation. You can have a good laugh."

"And if you're shy—as a person, I mean—then acting's perfect," Simon said.

"*Not* shy, don't you mean?" asked Tricia. "Surely it's the exact opposite of shyness, this desire to get up on the stage and display yourself."

"But you never do," said Simon. "Display yourself, I mean. Hiding in another person's character, their clothes, hairstyle, everything. You can be almost unrecognizable on the stage. I think it's the main attraction: putting on someone else's personality. You can hide most of yourself, if you're crafty."

"But not all of yourself," Chris smiled. "Bits of you will keep creeping in, you know, like your voice and the way you move, and certain indefinable things that are as personal to you as your fingerprints."

"Well, OK, yeah," Simon said. "Sure. All that. Still, I reckon the stage is a good place to hide."

"I like it," said Dinah, "because if you're acting, you're special. You're yourself and something extra as well. People can admire you."

"I like the idea of transforming myself," Mike said. "I like dressing up. And I like the safety."

"Safety?" We all looked at him in total confusion.

"Yes. I think that's why most people like the theater. The company and the audience. The company because it's comforting to have a short time during which every word you say and every move you make has been set down and determined by someone else: writer or director. It means that for those few hours, the responsibility for what you are doing or saying is lifted. You are safe. You are Vershinin. Vershinin does this, stands like that, speaks like this, loves Masha, leaves the town, is sad—and all without actually affecting you, yourself, in the slightest. It's marvelous. You can rant and scream and faint and kill and let your emotions out of their cages quite safely. They won't bite anyone. They're just shadows."

Chris said: "I get it. 'A tale full of sound and fury/ Signifying nothing.' "

Tricia smiled. "Sound and fury maybe. But not signifying nothing. It's got to mean something or no one would keep coming."

"They also come for safety in a way though," I said. "I know what Mike means, I think. People go to the theater to be lifted out of their real lives for a bit."

"And even if what they're lifted into is a kind of real life of its own," Charlie said, "at least it's not *their* life, their troubles, their characters. And they're only in it for a couple of hours, aren't they?"

"They'll be walking out of our *Three Sisters* during the first twenty minutes," said Chris, "if we don't get back and work on it—right now."

We groaned, and drained cups of tea and coffee grown cold. Then we made our way back to the empty gray stage, ready to transform it by our presence into the Prozorovs' house, on a morning in May.

Working on it: it sounds very "all hands on deck" and "everyone pulling together" and for much of the time that was exactly how it was. Sometimes, though, there were hours, even days, when nothing went right at all. There were times when it was almost impossible to coordinate hands and feet to get you around the set without bumping into the furniture, and when every word you spoke was flat and boring, like Coke with the fizz gone out of it. I didn't have many such times, it's true, but there was the occasion when, as Chris put it, I had about as much life in me as a stuffed parrot. I was supposed to be being bossy, sugar-sweet and nasty with it, dismissing the sisters' old nanny and generally throwing my weight around.

"It's all got to be there, Mel," Chris said, "when you enter. It's got to be there at the same time: vanity and a kind of fake compassion for Masha and Olga and concern about the fire, and the desire to get things in the house organized your way . . ."

"Yes, but . . ." I said, nearly in tears having been through the scene eight times, "it's like having a bloody kaleidoscope on my neck and not a face. I seem to have to change expression every ten seconds."

"No, don't be ridiculous, Mel, you can't do that. Try and think of the character in layers: selfish first. Feel it. Then, behaving like a good sister. Then, right on top, the top layer, the splendid self-assurance. The lack of doubt. The belief that what you're doing is right."

I tried again. And again. It got worse and worse. In the end, even the words had disappeared out of my head, and as I stood silently in the middle of the stage trying to tidy them in my mind into some kind of speaking-order, I heard Chris sighing loudly to himself in the first row of the stalls. That was it. I felt as if a huge fountain of misery that I'd been keeping pushed down for the last hour had suddenly gushed up inside me. I ran as fast as I could to the Green Room where I flung myself onto a sofa and began to howl and weep.

"Mel." It was Mike. "Mel, don't cry. Honestly. Stop crying, please."

"Go away. I don't want you to see me with my face like this. I don't want anyone."

"It's Mike."

"I know. I wish you'd go away and leave me alone."

He knelt down beside the sofa and began to stroke my hair as if I were a small child.

"You don't mean that. Come on. Look up. Go on, I dare you."

"I can't. I look awful. My nose is running."

"Here's a hankie. Now sit up."

I looked at him from under lids I knew were puffed up and disgusting. I could have hugged him for not laughing at me. I sat up, and took his hankie and began to mop myself up.

"Thanks, Mike," I said. "I'm sorry . . . about being silly, and your hankie and everything. I'll give it back when it's been washed."

"The hankie doesn't matter. It's you. What is it, Mel?"

"What do you mean, what is it? Didn't you hear him? Sighing like that at me, as if I were completely useless, and that's after we've been going over that scene for an hour. Oh, I could spit, I could really."

"Yes, of course I heard him. I should think everyone did, but it's nothing personal. He was just getting fed up, that's all."

"Yes, I know. Fed up with me."

"No, *not* fed up with you. Just sick of having to go over it again and again. Same as you."

"But I don't sigh, do I?"

"You should then, if it'll make you feel better. Anyway, we haven't got time for people to go off into the Green Room and cry. That's being temperamental."

"Heaven forbid!" I muttered and stood up to look in the mirror. Temperament was not allowed—my mother had made that abundantly clear. You had to be a trouper, which meant taking criticism on the chin, being yelled at and still producing a smile, and all in all behaving like a fully fledged saint.

"Tell Chris," I said to Mike, "that I shall come and do that scene again in a minute. I must just find some way of disguising these eyes of mine."

"Have a cup of coffee with me and your eyes'll be OK in a couple of minutes."

"Your faith is touching," I said.

After fifteen minutes or so, I felt better.

"Let's go back now," I said. "Do I look all right?"

"You've looked fine to me all along," Mike answered.

"You're kidding."

"No, honestly. You have," he said and took my hand and pulled me up off the sofa. I followed him down to the stage, feeling happy. He must love me, I thought. Only someone who loved me could be as blind as that. It would be good to report that having got all that crying out of my system, I then went straight on and did the scene to perfection, but not a bit of it. I did it half a dozen times again that day, and never got it right. It fell into place quite suddenly a few days later, when I was thinking of something else. Wouldn't you just know it?

From the time that Clare left the company, it seemed that we entered, all of us, into a kind of slide toward the first night. Rehearsals, which were already hard work and quite intensive to my way of thinking, became even more detailed with Chris lying in wait to pounce on one false movement or gesture.

"Until your costumes are ready," he told us one day, "I want all the girls in skirts for rehearsal, please. The longest you've got. You simply cannot move in a nineteenth-century way in jeans. You are all doing the wrong thing with your feet and knees."

The next day saw us in an odd assortment of pleated school skirts and long cotton Indian garments that had seen better days. Louise made the mistake of turning up in an ankle-length tube which hobbled her knees to such a degree that she could barely totter across the stage.

"What," said Chris, "do you call *that*, Louise?"

"It's a skirt. You said we should wear skirts."

"The way you're walking in it, it looks like an instrument of torture. Honestly, Louise, where's your sense? Couldn't you have worn something else?"

Louise, nettled by Chris's tone, shouted down into the auditorium at him:

"It's the only bloody skirt I've got, unless you want me up here in a denim mini. I'm not buying a new skirt on your account and that's flat. We're not all made of money, you know."

"Sorry, Louise," said Chris. "Keep your hair on. I certainly didn't mean to suggest you buy another skirt. Carry on in that one, and Mel, be a sport and run up to Ruby and see if she's got something for Louise to drape herself in, just for now. Silly of me, really. She's probably got skirts up there to fit all of you. I should have thought of it. Quick as you can. Everybody else back in the auditorium. Louise, Tricia, and Dinah on stage. Louise, go back to *'Dear sisters, I want to make my confession.'* "

I said the scene over to myself in my head as I went up to see Ruby. Was I not, after all, the understudy? When I got to the bit that says: *"You read some novel and you think, that's all old stuff, everyone knows that. But as soon as you fall in love you realize that no one knows anything and that we each have to solve our own lives . . ."* I was so shaken by the truth of the words that I stood on the landing for a full thirty seconds, amazed that Chekhov should have expressed so exactly what I felt. It was just like Tennyson and the Brook poem: an accurate description.

"Anton, baby," I said aloud to the walls and banisters, "you *said* it!" (I should mention, perhaps, that I had not lost my reason at this point. I often speak out loud. It is the consequence of being an only child with just myself for company during my formative years.) I put my head round the door and called:

"Ruby?"

"She's not here, dear. Can I help you?"

I thought: I'd know that mouse-voice anywhere. It was Dinah's mother, metamorphosed by the donning of a flowered overall into a Member of the Backstage Staff. She smiled at me.

"Hello. It's you, Mel, dear. It *is* nice to see you. We haven't seen you for ever such a long time."

"We're fantastically busy . . ."

"I know. I didn't realize, really, what a lot of work it all is. I'm learning ever so much. You never think, do you, that every bit of clothing you see has got to be got ready for each person. Look what I'm doing now: machining rows of this lace onto Olga's blouse, which is really a plain one of Ruby's. I'm sorry, listen to me rattling on . . . did you want something?"

"I wanted to borrow a long skirt for Louise to wear on stage. Just for rehearsal, so something that won't matter too much."

"Oh, we've got hundreds of long skirts. Look." She pointed to a rail crowded with hangers on which were pinned rather tatty-looking skirts in noncolors like dun and washed-out black and hessian brown. This had evi-

126

dently been a production of some austerity with a cast of thousands of female peasants. I took the nearest skirt to me (a poison-green number) and held it up against my waist.

"Louise is much the same size as I am. It should be OK."

"There's elastic at the waist," Mrs. McLaren agreed. "It'll fit anyone. That's the thing with theatrical costumes. They've got to be adaptable."

Ruby had been talking to her, you could see that. I said, to be polite:

"Is Mr. McLaren managing all right in the shop, without you and Dinah? He must be ever so busy all by himself."

For a split second you could see Mrs. McLaren *actually trying to remember* who Mr. McLaren was and what the sweetshop was, so thoroughly had she immersed herself in the life and doings of a theatrical Wardrobe Mistress.

Then she answered: "Yes . . . he's fine . . . well, of course he is extra busy, what with it being school holidays and everything . . . but it's only for this once, isn't it? And I do feel badly about that poor—what's her name?—Clare, is it? Ruby told me all about it." Mrs. McLaren lowered her voice. "It seems she had a row with the director. Ruby didn't make it clear what it was, but I believe it was some sort of lovers' tiff . . ."

I nodded silently. She didn't know anything, that much was clear. Dinah had obviously said not one word to her mother on the subject of Chris. It struck me again (because it had often struck me before) how little some people tell their parents. I tell my mother nearly everything. Perhaps it's being an only child (you can make that excuse for a hell of a lot, if you try hard enough) or maybe I'm a blabbermouth, or it could be as my mother says, and a lot of people have what is known as "a communication problem."

127

"I'd better get back on stage now," I said. "It's good to see you. You'll be coming down with Ruby the day after tomorrow, to try out all the costumes, won't you?"

"Ooh, yes, I can't wait for that. I'm longing to see it. It sounds that sad from up here. I've seen Ruby having a quiet sniff more than once. We turn the tannoy on sometimes, just to have a listen, but it's all in bits and out of order, isn't it? It'll be different when it's done right through from beginning to end."

"Yes . . . thanks . . . I must go now. 'Bye." I said, and flew back to the stage, well aware that I'd taken far too long. Chris wasn't worrying about Louise's skirt any longer, however. He was now laying into Simon, Mike, Johnny, and Derek.

"You are *not* alcoholic breakdancers. You are *not* juvenile acrobats. You are not hooligans or layabouts or street-wise *anything*. You are SOLDIERS. Do you understand? Military men, not sniveling little schoolboys. You are to stand and walk only like soldiers. You are buttoned into tight uniforms, damn it . . . and if any of you doesn't know what soldiers look like or how they move, I'm going to get George, who was in the Army about a hundred years ago, to drill you for two hours a day in the parking lot. Get it? Now start again. And for Pete's sake, put your shoulders back and pretend your legs are made of something other than India rubber. OK?" The soldiers nodded, and shuffled to the wings ready to try again.

Mike and I were together during that time for almost every hour of the day, and quite late into the evening. Together and not together. He would come and sit beside me in the auditorium, while we were both not needed on stage, and if the house lights were down, which they often were, we would kiss, and then break guiltily, afraid of having missed

128

something of importance, and also unwilling to make a spectacle of ourselves in front of everybody—even though everybody knew how things were between us. Except me. Mike had never said anything to me about love. Not one word. This was not something I could bring myself to discuss with anyone. I didn't want to admit it, in case it was considered so unusual as to be abnormal. I thought: it's a kind of shyness. He must at least like me a lot, or he wouldn't kiss me, or put his arm around me when we're walking in the street, or be with me whenever he could. And he wouldn't stand in the wings, all tense and brooding, when I was kissing Matt at the end of Act One. I was getting quite good at that. It was doubtless the extra practice I'd been putting in with Mike. One day, I asked him directly. I said:

"You don't like it when I'm kissing Matt, do you?"

"No." (Looking at the ceiling. My, those follow-spots are suddenly amazingly interesting!)

"Why not? It's only acting. It doesn't mean anything."

"I know, it's just . . ."

"What?"

"I'm jealous."

"Really? Why?"

"Well, when you kiss Matt there, it looks as if you're enjoying it. As if you love him."

"But I'm *pretending* to love him. I'm ACTING."

"Acting bloody well, if you ask me . . ."

"Well," I answered reasonably enough, I thought, "what about you, then?"

"What about me?"

"You look to me as if you're in love with Masha, anguished to be leaving her. What about your kiss in Act Four? I'm supposed to sit through it without batting an eyelid, is that it?"

Mike looked genuinely shocked. "But . . ." He could hardly find words. "I think of you, didn't you know that? I pretend it's you I'm kissing. Truly. I do."

"I believe you," I said, "if you say so, but why is it that you're pretending and not that I am? Why are you acting when I'm not?"

Mike mumbled something vaguely apologetic under his breath and was then luckily summoned up on stage. I thought for a moment about what he'd said. Well, yes, I decided, some of it was pretending. I did partly get through the scene by imagining it was Mike I was kissing, certainly at the beginning. Still, as I grew more accustomed to kissing Matt (and under the critical eye of Chris and the assembled hordes) I did begin to enjoy it a bit for its own sake, in a kind of educational way. I found it fascinating that two boys should be so different: different smells, mouths, teeth, bodies. It was almost as if they'd been made from entirely separate substances. And even more interesting was the difference in me as I kissed each of them. With Matt I was always fully aware: of him, of me, of what Louise must be thinking, of where we were and where all the other people were, too. My feet were set squarely on the stage and I knew just what was going on. When Mike kissed me, parts of me felt as if they were going down a slide in the dark, rushing away from me, and I lost all sense of what other bits of me (my brain, for example) were doing. I came to the conclusion that because I didn't love Matt, I could, as it were, float pleasantly on the surface of his kisses, whereas with Mike, all the love I felt washed over my head like waves each time he touched me, drowning everything else out entirely.

I've just been thinking (looking out of the window and sucking the end of my pen) how strange it would be to come home from school one day, or from work, and open your front door to find that every bit of furniture (and carpets, lamps, pictures: the lot) had disappeared. The house you lived in would no longer be *your* house. It would be nothing but a skeleton or a container waiting to be filled with someone's life. You have to be a certain kind of person to be able to imagine what this series of empty rooms will look like when the carpets are down and the curtains are up, and this chair is put here and that one there, and so forth. After Clare left, I often remembered the model she had made of the Prozorovs' house, and the thought that it had been sent to the bottom of George's dustbins made me sad in ways I couldn't really understand.

Then the day came when Pete and his helpers, Gill and Keith, came up from the bowels of the earth and everybody spent the whole morning putting up the set, checking that all the flats slid on and off stage smoothly, making sure that doors and windows opened and closed properly, slowly transforming the acting area into a scaled-up version of Clare's model. Best of all was what Chris called "dressing the set": deciding where the potted plants, carpets, lamps, pictures, antimacassars, and cushions would go. Chris was like an interior decorator, getting it all just right. "Try that cushion on the red chair, Mel, and let's see how it looks . . . no, I don't like that. Put it on the chaise lounge. Is that better? I'm not sure. Leave it there for the moment, and we'll see in rehearsal . . . it might get in Vershinin's way in Act Two. Anyway, let's leave it there for now. Pete, is there any way of getting that candlestick to shine a little less? It's going to catch the lights and flash in people's eyes like a lighthouse. Tricia, try pulling that curtain six inches to the left. I think the people sitting in this block of seats can see a bit too much of the backstage area . . ." For hour after hour that day, we arranged and rearranged, moved and moved again, put up and took down, until at last Chris was happy and we were all completely exhausted.

"Tomorrow," Chris explained triumphantly to the drooping bodies draped over the first three rows of the stalls, "we'll have a costume fitting in the morning and in the afternoon we'll walk through the whole play for the lighting cues and check that the chairs do actually hold the people who have to sit on them. Stuff like that. Also, there'll be photographers from the local paper to do the Front of House photos. OK? Great. You've all worked like mad and I'm truly grateful. It looks terrific, doesn't it?"

We buzzed agreement at him, and I was a bit miffed that he didn't so much as mention Clare's contribution to the general wonderfulness of all the décor he was so happy with.

"Looks good, doesn't it?" Mike whispered. The Act Four set was up at the moment, with the repainted avenue of firs looking just right.

I said: "No thanks to us."

Mike grinned at me. "Costumes tomorrow. Uniforms and boots. I can't wait."

"Boys!" I said. "Honestly! Never think about anything except your appearance, do you?"

"*Is* there anything else?" Mike said. "And I'll bet you look a stunner in your smart green belt, too." He nodded toward the stage. "That all makes it look . . . true, doesn't it? We're actually going to do it, aren't we? I'm scared to death, to tell you the honest truth. Do you think it's too late to drop out? I can't go up there and be Vershinin in front of all those people."

"You'll be OK," I said, "once you start. It's only stage-fright. It'll pass. Come to the Green Room."

"I know," Mike said on the way out of the auditorium, "but I'll tell you something. It's not pleasant. It makes me understand what my mother must feel. A little of what she feels, anyway."

That evening, my mother said:

"I've been to see Mike's mum. She's quite nice, isn't she? It must be awful for her."

"Did she say she'd come with you? To the first night?"

"Well, no, she didn't actually *say* she would, but I think I'll be able to persuade her. She's really anxious to see it. I told her over and over again I'd help her, and not leave her for one second. I reckon she might come."

"It's only three days away now," I said, and as I said it, I felt a wobbling and trembling in my stomach. "I'm scared to bloody death, Mum," I said. "Whatever shall I do?"

My mother was most unsympathetic. "That's part of it," she said. "Part of the excitement, that terror. It'll pass. It's just to make the adrenaline go around faster."

"Mine's going round quite fast enough, thank you."

"You'll be all right on the night, dear," my mother said. Theatrical Cliché Number Four, I thought, and what a lot of rubbish. Who knows whether I'll be all right or not? I had a terrible momentary vision of the top of my head opening up, and all my lines (Natasha's and the three sisters') flying out like a thousand blackbirds, while I clawed the air, trying to catch hold of some of them and bring them back. I dismissed this bleak picture and replaced it with my favorite fantasy: Someone Devastatingly Important just happens to be passing, comes in, is bowled over by my performance, comes backstage, takes me off to London, the National Theatre, the Barbican, TV, movies, Oscar ceremonies, etc., etc. This fantasy was no longer as convincing as it used to be. At the beginning of the rehearsal period, it had been (just) possible to imagine that I could reach the dizzy heights of perfection in my performance. Now, I knew what I knew, and the fantasy became more and more farfetched. And having such dreams at all (if I were to be honest with myself) was so common as to be counted Theatrical Cliché Number Five.

Ruby and Mrs. McLaren moved in next morning and Joyce from the Box Office came, too, to help with the whole abracadabra business they were engaged in. They pinned and sewed and turned up and put down. They made sure buttons were firm and epaulettes didn't tremble. They added scarves and brooches, artificial flowers, shawls, gloves, and then sat back and looked at us as we paraded about the stage for Chris to approve. Dinah's mother was enjoying herself hugely, just like one of the gang, except of course, she avoided Dinah as much as she could. Dinah had decided to try and make people forget that she had any connection with the timid little woman in the flowered overall, who just happened to be helping out.

I looked at the others. I couldn't believe it. They were no longer themselves. They moved differently. The girls, their heads held up because of the high-necked blouses they were wearing, rustled their skirts as they walked, and sat elegantly on the edges of chairs, and took smaller steps.

Louise had put her red hair into a bun at the back of her neck. She kept touching it, and glancing down at the lace crusts on the cuffs of her blouse.

"It feels funny, doesn't it?" she said. "All this stuff. I don't feel like me anymore."

"I know," I said. "I don't either. That's the whole idea. It's magic."

"Yeah, great," Louise said, and went to talk to Ruth and Charlie. She'd misunderstood me. I didn't mean "magic" in the colloquial sense to stand for "terrific" or "super" or "great." I meant it literally. Real Magic. Real transformations. The boys were, if anything, even more startlingly changed than the girls: more grown-up, standing with stiff backs in their military jackets and practicing striding about like soldiers in their boots.

"I feel shy of you," I said to Mike. "You look much—"

"Taller?"

"No, I was going to say 'wider' . . . more substantial."

"And you, my dear," said Mike, twirling an imaginary moustache, "look deliciously vulgar in that green belt. How delightfully tight your bodice is!"

"Too tight, do you think?"

135

"No, just right."

Ruby had done me proud as far as the belt went. It was the vilest shade of lime green and shiny to boot, made out of a satiny sort of material. It hung down at the back like a sash, guaranteed to produce conniptions in anyone who had ever been anywhere near stylish old Moscow. I was giving a great deal of thought to the kind of makeup Natasha should wear, to do her clothes full justice. A heavy hand with the blusher would be called for, I concluded.

We kept our costumes on for the afternoon, as we walked through the play over and over again for Tim in the lighting box to work his particular enchantments. Summer light and autumn, daylight, twilight, two o'clock in the morning candlelight, everything was possible. At the flick of a switch, lamps brightened and dimmed, colors shone out from the sides of the stage, from above our heads, from the back of the auditorium, and as they altered, so the look of the set did, too, and the room that had a moment ago been flooded with May sunshine for Irina's name day was now full of velvety shadows in the lamplight.

At the end of the day Chris said: "You are all to sleep till at least noon tomorrow, and to come in for the Dress Rehearsal at five o'clock. Please do not forget your make-up, girls. Nothing too elaborate, please, this is only a small theater. Foundation, eyes, lips, blusher. Ruth, I've got ageing makeup for Anfisa in the men's makeup box upstairs. Lads, you don't have to worry—Gill will see to you, and make sure you're the right colors and you don't shine. Roland, if you could get here a bit earlier, your wig's arriving in the morning, so we'll have to try it on early and give you a chance to get accustomed to it. OK, that's about it. Get a good night's sleep and eat a decent meal before you come in."

If, I thought, my stomach will settle down in one place for long enough.

A slow rain had begun to fall by the time I left the theater. The light that was neither proper daylight nor proper darkness turned everything to the color of bruises. The brick parcels that had looked so neat and cheerful not so long ago had been opened and bricks lay scattered about in random-looking heaps all over the place. More cement mixers had appeared: outer space shapes in a lunar landscape, their open mouths dark and silent. I turned my coat collar up and fixed my eyes resolutely on the headlights of all the cars moving on the main road through the dismal twilight, homeward-bound, and walked quickly toward the bus stop.

OK, folks! Look out, here it comes—Theatrical Cliché Number Six: a bad dress rehearsal means a good first night. In this instance the cliché actually had some truth in it. Even now, after all this time, I don't like thinking about the dress rehearsal. It gives me the collywobbles just to remember it. Disasters included:

1) Roland sitting rather heavily on the best chair and breaking the right front leg.

2) Louise putting her foot through the fabric of her dress and tearing a huge great split in it almost from waist to hem.

3) Dinah losing her false eyelashes. (Well, she thought it was a disaster and cried and carried on as if it were the end of the world.)

4) Tricia's bus breaking down and Tricia not arriving

at the theater until five minutes before the curtain. (This was the one that nearly finished me off.)

5) Mike drying up completely—forgetting his words not once, not twice, but three times.

6) A flat falling flat on to the stage, nearly flattening Simon. (The avenue of firs—right on!)

7) Lights not going on when they were supposed to, and shining out like beacons when they were meant to be off.

8) People walking on and off stage through all the wrong entrances and exits, just as though we hadn't all been over it a thousand times.

9) People paralyzed by giggles, corpsing all over the place, and generally at the most poignant moments of the action.

10) And this was worse than any of the nine other disasters put together—all of us stumbling through the play like zombies, scarcely even speaking audibly, let alone actually acting.

I admired Chris for the restraint he showed while giving us our notes. He seemed to think there was hope for us yet. I seriously doubted it. So, it seemed, did Louise, Dinah, Tricia, and Ruth, who shared a dressing room with me. They'd all taken off their stage clothes ("Just hang the costumes up on the rail, my dears, as soon as you can," Ruby had said) and were sitting in front of the bulb-studded mirrors, moaning.

"Everyone's going to be able to see that tear" (Louise).

"What if I burst out laughing tomorrow, when I'm supposed to be remembering my father's death?" (Tricia).

"I hope they fix that stupid flat. It nearly killed Simon" (Me).

"Where did I put my Anfisa headscarf? Have you put it in your bag, Mel, by mistake?" (Ruth).

"I've forgotten every single word I've got to say. If I had to go on now and do it, I wouldn't know where on earth to begin" (Me).

"Has anyone got any cotton wool?" (Dinah).

"My whole family's coming. I can't stop them from coming now. Ooh, I wish I could get ill" (Louise).

"Don't you dare, I can't do your part" (Me).

"Yes, don't you dare. I can't do Mel's part" (Ruth).

On and on the voices rose and fell against the bare gray walls of the room. In the end, everyone had gone except Ruth and me. I hadn't even taken off my Act Four dress yet. It was a splendidly vulgar affair in a strident tartan: all yellows and sharp reds and greens. I looked, I thought, like a tin of shortbread on legs.

"Change quickly," Ruth said, as I took this outfit off. "Charlie's coming to fetch me in a minute. We're going to forget all of this—" she waved a hand around and nearly sent Dinah's monstrous regiment of bottles careering to the floor, "and go and see a movie somewhere. Do you and Mike feel like coming? I think Simon and Derek said they wanted to."

I felt very affectionate toward Ruth all of a sudden, and full of admiration for the knack she and Charlie had of pulling everyone else in around them into the warm circle of their company, even though they were a couple. Other couples, like Chris and Dinah, Louise and whoever she was with (it was becoming harder and harder to tell) and even Mike and I, kept the rest of the world out.

"Thank God," I said, "for you and Charlie. And for Roland and Tricia." Mercifully, Charlie walked in then, so I was saved from explanations.

He said: "Haven't you got all your guck off yet? Heavens, woman, a person can grow old waiting for you to dress."

139

"This guck," said Ruth, "is new guck I am putting on. The old guck is long gone."

"What a relief! And you, young Mel, how are you spending this fateful night?"

"Shaking violently in my bedroom, I expect."

"What? And is the gallant Mike not springing to the rescue?"

"He . . . he has to be at home tonight," I said, "and anyway, he'll probably be shaking, too."

"Why don't you," said Charlie leering at me with a Groucho Marx waggle to his eyebrows, "shake together? Now there's a novel concept. You should try it. You might quite enjoy it."

"Shut up, Charlie," said Ruth mildly, "and don't be so filthy. Not everyone's like you."

"More's the pity," said Charlie. "Well, never mind, this time tomorrow the first night will be well under way and then we can all look forward to the party afterwards, can we not? Wild and abandoned revelry on all sides . . . ho, ho. You and Mike *are* coming to that, aren't you?"

"Oh, yes," I said, "I wouldn't miss that for anything." As I spoke, I thought of Clare, missing everything, not seeing how it all worked out, how everything looked, and I knew I had to try, had to persuade her to come.

"Excuse me, you two," I said, "I have to make a very urgent phone call . . ." I ran from the room and two at a time down the stairs to the pay phone near the Box Office. As I was scrabbling in my purse for change and looking for my address book, I suddenly thought: what the hell, I'll use Chris's phone. It's the least he can do for Clare. The theater can pay for the call, I don't care. I crept into his office. I knew he'd be locked up with Tim in the lighting box for hours, and even if he did catch me, I wasn't doing anything wrong. I dialed the number.

"Hello, is that Clare?"

"Yes, who's that?"

"It's Mel. Mel Herbert, you know. Natasha."

"Hi, Mel, how are you? I've been thinking about all of you all day. Are you excited?"

"I'm terrified. Clare, tomorrow is the first night."

"I know."

"Well?"

"Well, what?"

"Are you going to come? See everyone? See the show? Come to the party . . . Oh, say you will . . ."

"I don't know, Mel. It's an awful long way. And I don't think . . . well, not everyone will be happy to see me."

"But *you* . . . what do you want to do?"

"I can't make up my mind and that's the truth."

"Try and come."

"I'll think about it. That's truly all I can say at the moment. I'll think about it."

"OK. And Clare?"

"Yes?"

"It looks lovely. It really does. The set and the clothes and everything. It's lovely."

"Good. I'm glad."

"I miss you."

"That's nice. I'll be back soon anyway. I'll come and visit you when I return. All right?"

"Right. Clare, are you designing *Othello?*"

I could hear the sigh over the phone. "I suppose so. I've resigned from Project, but well, I'd sort of promised so I'll have to do it, I think. And I want to do it in some ways."

"What about Dinah?"

"Nothing really. I shall have to come to terms with her, that's all. Perhaps I could design her a really hideous costume." She giggled.

141

I said, "You can laugh about it, Clare. You must be getting over it a bit. You *must* come up and see *Three Sisters*."

"I can laugh about it from three hundred miles away. I don't know how hilarious it'll be there on the spot."

"OK, I won't nag you any more."

"It's good to hear from you. Good luck for the first night."

"Thanks. See you."

"Yes, see you."

I put the receiver down feeling slightly cheered. Even if she didn't come for the show, Clare would soon be back. For a moment I fantasized her sweeping down tomorrow into the front row of the orchestra on the arm of a disgustingly handsome man, not giving a damn for anyone, least of all Chris and Dinah. It didn't seem very likely, even as a fantasy. I dismissed it from my mind.

I left the theater as darkness was falling.

"First thing tomorrow, miss," said George. As if I didn't know. "Marvelous things, first nights used to be: flowers for the leading lady, telegrams all round the mirrors, gentlemen of the press (that's the critics), all the cream of society in evening dress, lovely sherry glasses tinkling in the bar at the intermission."

"Poor old George!" I said. "It's coffee in the intermission and an audience of our family and friends mostly, I expect. I don't think the press will come, do you? Only the locals, anyway."

"Never mind, miss," George said, "it's a grand show for all that, and I wish you all luck with it."

"Have you seen it?"

"Oh, yes," said George, "we've been in and out these past few weeks, my broom and me, and we've seen most of it. In bits and pieces, like. It's a grand play." He sniffed.

I said: "I thought you liked more cheerful things. Things with dancers in them."

George smiled. "I'm not one to say no to dancers, that's true. But I like a good story. Don't hold with all this not knowing what's going on or who anyone is that goes on nowadays. Now Chekhov . . . that's what I call a good meaty play. And why? I'll tell you why. It's about real people. People like us." He clamped his mouth shut as if that were the very last word on the subject.

"Good night, George," I said.

"Good night, miss," George called after me. "You'll like the first night. Wait and see."

I've never been operated on in the hospital, and I've never been married, but I think I can imagine how I might respond if I were faced with the prospect of these two things coming up in the near future. Waking up on the morning of a first night is a distillation of the feelings associated with those two events. It's a combination of terror, excitement, pure happiness, sickness in the pit of the stomach, curiosity, and an inability to eat anything. There is also about the morning of a first night (as about a wedding or a trip to hospital) the undeniable fact that YOU are the center of attention: you're mollycoddled, fussed, petted, loved, and generally worried about. My mother even decided to close her shop for the afternoon "to help you get ready, love." That was how she put it, even though there was nothing to do but hang around drinking endless cups of coffee and silently going over, yet again, lines that seem tangled around in your head like wires in the bowels of an ancient radio. There was also the pleasure of wondering whether you would get anything from anyone. I'd already been given, by my mother, a splendid makeup case divided into more compartments than the Orient Express. She'd also tried to persuade me to take in a fancy, kimono-style garment with peonies rioting all over the sleeves. "To put your makeup on in, dear," she said, but I pointed out gently but firmly that a) I was not Talullah Bankhead and b) I was sharing a huge dressing room with other people. Indeed, that the Project didn't have one with a big, silver star pinned on the door. (Theatrical Cliché Number Seven!)

"So what'll you wear as a gown?" my mother wanted to know.

"The shirt I got from Oxfam." (Fifty pence. A man's blue shirt. I was very fond of it.) I appealed to the superstitious side of her nature. "It is," I announced, "my lucky shirt."

"Well, then, *of course* you must wear that and nothing else!"

I had sent two good-luck cards: one for the men's dressing room and one for the ladies'. I'd also bought Mike a special present: a small fluffy creature with round eyes and no other features, whom I named Humphrey. But what if he'd bought me nothing? I didn't want to embarrass him by producing Humphrey (gift-wrapped into the bargain) if he was empty-handed. And yet I *did* want Mike to know that I'd thought of him, bought him something. This knotty problem exercised the jelly that had slipped into my head in place of my mind at regular intervals throughout the day.

I had a very long bath (cf. A Wedding). I chose my clothes for the party after the show with great care. Folded them neatly into a suitcase (cf. Going to the Hospital). Remembered shoes at the last minute. Went over my makeup case to check I hadn't forgotten anything. Put Humphrey in. By the time I was ready, I felt as though I were about to emigrate to Australia, and it wasn't anywhere near time to go to the theater.

I find Time extremely irritating. It has an unfortunate habit of slowing down to slug-crawl speed just when you want it to race by, like now, when there was absolutely nothing to do but wait and stare out of the window and twiddle your thumbs until you could reasonably leave the house. I had long ago decided that I wasn't going to get to the theater "on the half"—half an hour before the curtain. I was going to get there at least an hour before we had to start. My mother offered to take me by car.

"I've got tons of time before I go and get Mike's mum. Honestly. And that suitcase weighs a ton."

"It's OK, really," I answered. "I'd rather go on the bus. Please."

"You vant," my mother put on her Greta Garbo voice, "to be alo-o-ne?"

"Got it in one," I said.

I enjoyed myself on the bus. I looked around at everyone else, feeling smug that I was going somewhere more exciting than they were. I was quite sorry, in fact, that none of them knew where I was going. I wished, at every bus stop, that someone I knew would get on, so that I could tell them (and the other hapless passengers) where I was off to in the ringing tones of The Theater. I got off the bus as ostentatiously as I could, hoping that at least some people might make the connection on account of my aura, which I felt to be deeply theatrical.

The first thing I noticed as I approached the Project was that someone had started building a wall on the wasteland. They'd stopped for a cup of tea, because the place was deserted, but there it was—a small slice of wall sticking up out of the earth. Someone had collected red bricks and put them together into a pattern, into the beginning of something—maybe even a house. Immediately, the chaos all around the wall took on a shape and a direction. It was possible to believe that all the scatterings and bits and pieces would one day grow into a real building. I was immensely cheered by this visible sign of order-out-of-chaos and decided that it was a lucky omen for our first night. I thought of telling the others and then I changed my mind. Actors, I knew, were supposed to be very superstitious, but this was probably going a bit far, even for them. I could keep, I thought, my omens to myself.

Box Office Joyce was busy in front of the theater, pinning up big, glossy photographs in the display boxes along the outside wall. She was already dressed to kill, in a black gown with sparkles in the material and newly crimped hair.

"Hello, dear," she called out. "You're a bit early, aren't you? Come and admire the photos. They've come out really well, I think."

They had come out well, I suppose, and yet it lowered my spirits to look at them. In them, everyone and everything looked unreal: stiff, posed, costumed, made-up. We looked like children dressing up for charades. The set looked like a set, the clothes seemed not to belong to us properly, and you could see lines of makeup quite clearly, especially on those people who had to be old, like Roland and Ruth. It was then I realized The Truth. It bounced off the sparkles on Joyce's dress and flashed among the blue waves of her hair: *it was only our speaking of the words in a certain way, our particular modes of being on that stage, that might turn a charade into something an audience could properly believe in, at least while they were watching.* What mattered was our aliveness, our physical presence. If it weren't for that, every theater in the world might just as well close its doors and leave matters to film and television. And film and television in their turn were made up of tricks and deceptions. Theater and the movies: they were like two different kinds of fabric held up to a window. Movie-illusion fabric was woven tightly. Hardly any peeps of light from the Real World penetrated the cloth. More often than not, you even forgot the presence of a camera. Theater-illusion fabric was practically lace: you could look through it and see almost the whole of the Real World. Or you could see very little. It depended on the way you looked, and on where the light was directed. Joyce put a stop to these musings.

"Come inside and I'll show you the programs. You can see your name in black and white."

"Yes, please," I said, and followed her into the foyer. I'd quite forgotten about programs.

"Heavens," I said when Joyce showed me the cast list. "There we all are." My name, all lined up in black capitals, seemed to have very little connection with the person I was. Looking at it gave me a strange feeling of distance from myself.

"Isn't the cover grand, though?" Joyce said. "Hasn't she done good likenesses of them?"

The picture on the pale green cover of the program was a pen-and-ink sketch of Olga, Masha, and Irina's faces. Unmistakably Clare's work.

"It's beautiful," I said. "It's just like them and sort of more than them, if you know what I mean. Oh, I do wish she could have been here."

"There, there, dear." Joyce put a motherly arm around my shoulder. "Don't you fret now."

"May I keep this?" I asked.

"Well, of course. A person's got to have such things to stick in their scrapbook."

"And can I have another one as well? To send to Clare? Or to keep for her till she comes back? Please, Joyce."

"Very well, dear. Seeing as it's for Clare . . . but you put them away in that case of yours or they'll all be round here wanting extra programs for their aunties and uncles and we simply haven't got enough."

"I won't breathe a word. Thanks ever so much, Joyce."

"You're welcome, and the very best of luck for tonight."

"Ta," I said. "Can I go through this way?" I pointed to the auditorium.

"Well, seeing as you're so early . . . go on."

George was in the auditorium with his vacuum cleaner, putting last-minute touches to the floor. He turned the machine off when he saw me and smiled.

"Scallywag! Who said you could come through this way?"

"Joyce did . . . oh, George, don't be cross."

"I'll try extra hard. You'd better go on up to your dressing room. Lots of nice little surprises up there, I shouldn't wonder."

"Surprises? Oh, George, you don't mean magnums of champagne for us to drink out of our satin slippers after the show, do you?"

"Cheeky monkey! Go and see. I'm not saying a word. Go on. Scram. I've got a first night tonight, even if you haven't. Scat."

"I'm going . . . keep your hair on."

"Good luck," George said and turned the vacuum cleaner on again before I could thank him.

It took fully five minutes for it to sink in. Our dressing room had changed into some sort of flowery dell overnight. It was hard to see where we were all going to put our makeup. George had had a field day, you could see that, putting all the bouquets into vases for us (and where did all the vases come from? I'd never seen them before), and arranging the cards beside them. Chris had sent roses. My mother had sent a mixed bunch; so had Dinah's mum and dad, and Tricia's. So had Louise's family. So had Ruth's. These were general, for all of us. Then, specific bouquets: Dinah had a bunch from someone called Florry, Louise had one from Andrew (but not from Matt), Tricia had one from Roland. Ruth had a potted plant from Charlie. I had a bunch of tiny pink carnations, and my heart leaped up when I saw it, because I knew, I just knew, it was from Mike. I was wrong. It was from Clare. I was pleased. Of course I was pleased. I told myself so over and over again, thinking grimly of gift-wrapped Humphrey in my suitcase, and inwardly swearing at Mike for being so bloody undemonstrative and unsentimental. I distracted myself by opening the cards, from our neighbors and from those of my friends who knew about the show, and sticking them in true theater fashion all around the edges of my mirror. Then I opened my suitcase and took out a towel. I knew you were supposed to lay all the makeup you were going to use neatly out on a towel—it was practically Theatrical Cliché Number Eight—but my heart wasn't in it. I was nervous, sad that Clare wasn't here, worried about whether Mike's mother was going to get here or not, and thoroughly miffed at Mike himself. It was at this moment that Ruby came in, carrying armfuls of white blouses, newly ironed for the first night, and Louise's neatly mended skirt.

"You're bright and early, dear," she smiled. "My goodness me, it's like bleedin' Drury Lane in here and no mistake. What smashing flowers! Just let me hang this lot up and I'll come and have a read of all the cards. And while I'm doing that, why don't you go up to Wardrobe and fetch down my little gift?"

"Ruby, you shouldn't have . . ." I began.

"People always say that when they mean where is it, I can't wait to get my paws on it. Well, you can relax, love. It's nothing as exciting as all that. It's more practical."

"I can hardly wait." I ran out of the dressing room, up the stairs, and into Wardrobe. There I found Dinah's mother ironing the men's shirts, and three gift-wrapped bottles which turned out to be Lucozade.

"Hello, Mrs. McLaren," I said. "Thanks for the lovely flowers. You should see our dressing room."

"That's all right, dear. I wish you luck. I don't know how you must feel, but I'm so nervous . . . well, not nervous exactly, it's more a sort of excitement . . . you drink plenty of Ruby's Lucozade, all of you. It'll give you energy.

"I expect Dinah'll be in soon . . . you must come and see us when this is all over. Keep in touch. It would be a pity if you never saw each other, wouldn't it?"

I mumbled something politeish and made my way downstairs with the Lucozade bottles cradled in my arms.

Dinah had arrived by the time I reached the dressing room. She'd not only arrived, but had already taken off her street clothes and was sitting staring into the mirror wearing a flowery, silky kimono-type gown over underwear that had ideas above its station. My bra and panties were underwear; Dinah's aspired to the status of lingerie. They were frothy with lace and very white indeed. I came to the conclusion that she had probably bought them, chosen them especially to impress the rest of us, dazzle Ruby and delight any visitors passing through, but perhaps having a lover meant you had to wear beautiful underwear every day. I thanked heaven that at least I was wearing my most respectable bra. There were times when I'd have been held together by a safety pin, but this was not one of them.

151

"Hi," she smiled. "Isn't it amazing?" She gestured to include the flowers, the cards, the Lucozade, and a couple of mysteriously wrapped parcels that had made their appearance while I'd been upstairs.

"Fantastic." It was hard to keep on being cross with Dinah with all this going on.

"One of the parcels is for you," she said. "Mel, before anyone else gets here . . . can't we . . . what is it they say? Bury the hatchet?"

"OK," I said. "I suppose so. I was just thinking that I'm too excited to stay cross with you. But I don't think much of the way you went for Chris . . . I don't. And I don't think you needed to hurt Clare. Still, if you love him . . ."

"Oh, I do," said Dinah lightly, and I knew in that moment that she didn't. Not really. I also knew that she couldn't, wouldn't ever be able properly to love anyone. She reminded me of a butterfly. She'd be rushing between one flower and another, always attracted to the next: the next bright color, the next handsome face. She couldn't help it. I said:

"OK, friends then."

She jumped up from her chair and draped her arms, soft, silky butterfly wings, around my neck.

"That's great," she said, hugging me. "That's the best omen possible for tonight." She went back to the mirror. "Aren't you excited? And aren't you going to open that parcel? I'm longing to see what's in it."

I opened it. It was from Mike. Inside was a clear plastic frame, holding a photograph of three rather plain young women. They were sitting in a garden on cane chairs. They were wearing long dark skirts and blouses with tight sleeves that puffed out at the shoulder. In the background you could see trees and the balcony of a house. A note from Mike said:

"Good luck, Mel. I asked my mother if I could give you this. These three sisters are my grandmother and two great-aunts (all dead long ago). They are sitting in the garden of their summer house in Poland, which must be quite like Russia, I think.

Love, Mike

PS Look at the avenue of firs behind them!"

"What is it?" Dinah peered across to my bit of the shared dressing table.

"A photo."

"That's a bit of a funny present. What of?"

"Three sisters."

"Oh, I get it. Let's have a look."

I passed the frame to Dinah.

"Goodness,' she said. "It must be ages old. Are we supposed to look like that?"

"No, not exactly . . . It's more sort of . . ."

Ruth, Louise, and Tricia came in at that moment, which was lucky, because I couldn't think of a word with which to finish my sentence. The photo was of real people, that was what was so good about it. That was why I was so touched that Mike had thought of giving it to me. Real people connected to Mike and also connected to our imaginary Olga, Masha, and Irina. I didn't understand the threads that bound all the different bits of this reality together, I just knew that they were there and was moved almost to tears by the very fact of them.

"I'll be back in a minute," I said, taking Humphrey from my case.

"But don't you want to see this picture of Dinah in the evening paper?" Ruth called out after me as I left the room.

"Later," I shouted back.

I ran down the corridor to Mike's dressing room.

"Is Mike there yet?" I banged on the door.

"Ooh," said Roland, "it's that Mel, boys, after our bodies again! Hide everything. You can come in, dearie."

I opened the door and looked round it. Mike was sitting at his bit of the dressing table pondering his moustache and a bottle of spirit gum.

"It's for you-hoo!" Charlie said to him.

"Hi," I said. "Can you step outside for a moment?" Wolf whistles and chortles greeted this remark.

"Not much time before the curtain," said Charlie. I glared at him, wishing I had something to throw.

"Why don't you," I suggested sweetly, "get knotted?"

"Shut up, Charlie," said Mike as he made his way to the door.

"Please, miss," said Charlie in a sniveling whine, acting the contrite schoolboy, "I never meant it, miss, I was joking, honest I was, miss."

I giggled. "Don't call us, Charlie," I said. "We'll call you."

Mike and I stood in the corridor. I said: "I brought you something, too. Only it's nothing like as good as your present. Your present's the best thing I've ever had. Thanks ever so much."

"I knew you'd like it. I liked it. As soon as I saw it, I knew that you should have it. What's this?"

"Open it and see."

He opened Humphrey's gift wrapping and grinned. "Great!" he said. "But what the hell's it supposed to be?"

"I don't know. But it's called Humphrey."

"Hi, Humphrey." He put his hands on my shoulders. "Thanks, Mel. . . Mel?"

"Yes?"

"I'm terrified."

"Me, too."

"I feel as if I'm drunk or something. All wobbly and up in the air."

"It'll be OK when we get going, Mike. You'll be marvelous, don't worry."

Janet's voice came to us over the tannoy: "This is your half-hour call, everybody. Half an hour, please. Half an hour."

"Crikey," Mike said, "is that all? I'd better go and get this moustache fixed on and powder my hair. Mel?"

"Yes?"

"Good luck and . . . thanks."

"Good luck." He turned to go, then turned to face me.

"Mel?'

"Yes?'

"D'you think your mother will do it? Will she bring my mum, do you reckon?"

"You betcha," I said, trying to put a confidence in my voice that I was far from feeling.

"There's a gap in the curtain, near Janet's chair in the Prompt Corner. You can see the audience through it. I've checked. I'll get down there five minutes before the curtain and see if I can spot them. Want to come?"

"OK. I'll go and get ready now."

"See you."

Janet's voice: "Five minutes, everyone. This is your five-minute call."

"I'm going down to the wings," I announced.

"But why?" said Louise. "It's another five minutes . . . Oh, God, I feel as if I've got no stomach."

"Me, too," said Tricia. "I can't even remember what I say first."

"Good luck," I said and left the room. I was glad to leave it. It had turned into a cage in there and we were all flapping around like agitated birds, whisking our long skirts about and patting our hair. Chris had come in and told us how wonderful we were all going to be. Ruby had come in to make sure everyone was properly fastened, with Dinah's mother (in a fair old tremble by now) at her side.

"Not you, too," said Janet as I arrived at the Prompt Corner. "Mike's here. What is this? Curtain's about to go up . . ."

"Just for a second," I whispered. "It's urgent. Really it is. You haven't even called beginners yet."

"I'm just about to." She spoke into the tannoy. "Beginners, please. Tricia, Louise, Dinah. On stage, please. Simon, Roland, and Derek, stand by, please."

Mike left the gap in the curtain.

"They're not there. You don't need to look, Mel. They're not there. Your mother is going to miss the first night because of my mother."

I looked at Mike, pale under his makeup. "It doesn't matter," I said. "She'll come tomorrow. I'm just sorry about your mum. Maybe my mother will persuade her to come another night."

"No." Mike looked out onto the stage where Tricia, Louise, and Dinah were arranging themselves. "It doesn't matter. I'm used to it really. Her not coming to things."

But I'm not, I thought angrily. My mum has come to everything: every single thing from the time I was an angel at the play-group Christmas show. Now she's missing my first night, MY FIRST NIGHT, for Mike's mother, who's not even a proper friend of hers. Tears of self-pity filled my eyes. Clare in London, my mother not here—it wasn't fair. Everyone else had bunches of assorted relations from far and wide and I had no one at all. Bloody hell, I hadn't even got a father. I was just thinking how unfair it was of him to go and die like that before I'd even met him, when the curtains opened and Tricia started speaking. The mixed terror and elation of that moment banished every other thought from my head. We'd begun.

It was only during the intermission that I had time to think, to say to myself: OK, you're in the middle of it now, how does it feel? I came to the conclusion that it was:

a) like going over Niagara Falls in a barrel, and

b) like being on some kind of Alice-in-Wonderland-type magic potion that expands the stage into a universe and distances the rest of the world, shrinks it almost to nothing.

Our dressing room was more like an aviary than ever. It seemed to me that everybody was speaking at once; little half-sentences drifted about, falling through the air like feathers:

"I thought I was going to pass out . . . did it really . . . you were going to . . . I nearly . . . but did you see the bit when . . . and Roland forgot . . . anyway I turned round and you never . . . is he in the audience? . . . not *The Guardian* . . . from Granada Television . . . he was marvelous . . . you were ever so . . . wasn't she? . . . but I'd never have guessed . . . I nearly died when . . . do I look OK? . . . Mel left lipstick on his . . . that bloody cushion . . . Lucozade . . . bet that was Lorraine who had to be taken out . . ."

Janet's voice sounded hollow and distant:

"Act Three beginners, please. Act Three beginners. Ruth and Tricia, on stage, please. Charlie and Mel, stand by. Act Three beginners."

I stood up and followed Ruth and Tricia down to the stage. I wished the stage lights would go on. I wished Act Three could begin. I wanted the luxury of being in another place: somewhere where the fact that my mother had missed my first night didn't matter a bit. And it doesn't matter, I told myself. Not really. There's the second, third, and last night still. They'll probably be better. Anyway, it was my mother, with her smell-of-the-greasepaint mentality, who went in for things like the Myth of the First Night. Thinking this made me sad on my mother's behalf . . . she would never, never forgive herself . . . she would regret it all her life . . . there was my cue. I walked out onto the stage, taking Mel and all her troubles off and shrugging them on to the floor like a heavy coat. I was no longer Mel. I was Natasha. I bustled. I said:

"They're saying they'll have to quickly set up a charity for the people who lost their homes in the fire. I think that's an excellent idea. We must always help the poor. It's the duty of the rich." (Oh, my, my, Natasha is thinking, haven't I come a long way from the days of the green belt . . . the days when I had simply no idea of how to behave . . . I've come a long way. I'm as good as you now, Olga. Better than you.)

The play unfolded. The avenue of firs flat was rolled onto the stage without mishap. Tusenbach was killed, Vershinin left Masha sobbing in the garden, the soldiers moved away, and the birds began their southward journey. Natasha made plans. The Doctor read his newspaper, muttering: *"It doesn't matter . . . it doesn't matter . . ."*

Tricia spoke the play's last words:

"If only we could know . . . if only we could know!" and suddenly applause was like a magic wand, waking us up, bringing us back from the lives we had led in the play to our real lives. We took five curtain calls and then went crazy. Everyone was shouting, kissing, and hugging anyone

they could get hold of. Pete and Gill and Keith and Tim and Janet appeared and so did Chris, and I heard it. I heard it for myself. Theatrical Cliché Number Nine was TRUE. Alleluia! Cries of "Darling you were marvelous/great/terrific/fabulous" (well OK, perhaps I didn't really hear the "darling") echoed all round the stage. Chris managed after some minutes to make himself heard. We kept quiet to see what he had to say:

"It was absolutely great, all of you." He was beaming. "You all surpassed yourselves and I'm really proud of every single one of you. Well done. Now we're going to have a bit of a celebration at the Capricorn when you're ready, so I'll see you all there. Please leave your dressing rooms as you'd like to find them tomorrow. And please, now that I've got you all together and before we all get too plastered or something, I'd like to ask you to come in fifteen minutes or so before the half tomorrow. I've got some notes to give all of you. OK? Don't forget. Right. Let the jollifications begin!"

I made my way slowly back to the dressing room while everyone else was still cavorting about on stage. I felt as though I'd just run a marathon: totally exhausted. I pushed open the door and saw my mother sitting in my chair. She sprang up when she saw me and came toward me with outstretched arms:

"Darling," she said, "you were marvelous!" (My mother can be relied upon to get her lines right!)

"But how do you know?" I whined, back to being five years old again. "You weren't even there."

"Not there?" My mother laughed. "You don't seriously think I'd miss your first night, do you?"

"But what about Mike's mum? We looked and looked for you. We never saw you."

159

"Ever heard of getting there late? We slipped in about half a minute after you'd started. I had a bit of a struggle with Mrs. Corderly, but we did it in the end. I reckon it's quite an achievement."

"You mean Mike's mum saw it, too?"

"Yes, of course. Loved every minute of it. Spent Act Four in floods of tears. She's in Mike's dressing room. I've got to take her home. I promised. You'll make sure Mike brings you back safe from this Cast party, won't you?"

"I don't think it's a Cast party exactly. Bit of a rave-up at the Capricorn, that's all. But I'll make sure he gets me home all right."

My mother nodded. I knew what she was thinking. The Capricorn was not exactly dinner at the Ivy and waiting till the early hours of the morning to see what the papers had to say . . . still . . .

"By the way," she said, over her shoulder as she left the room, "I saw Clare. I thought you'd told me she'd run away to London with a broken heart?"

"Clare? Are you sure? It couldn't be. It must be a mistake."

"No, really, I'm sure it was her. She'll probably be at the party. 'Bye." I had scarcely had time to digest this piece of information when everyone else erupted into the room on a wave of shrieks and giggles. All the aviary birds were ready to shed one set of plumage and put on another.

"How you'll all get out of here looking decent," Ruby muttered (she'd come in as well), "is a mystery to me. I suppose I should be grateful your clothes are in one piece. Come on, girls, on the hangers, please. Slowly does it."

Clare was not in the Capricorn. Everyone else was. As a company, we must have generated clouds of steam because the windows were all fogged up and people looked sweaty. I felt flat. Anticlimactic. Also guilty for feeling so unpartylike when everyone else was in a mood of celebration. I sat drinking my punch with Mike and Louise and Andrew. Louise and Andrew didn't seem to be able to keep their hands off each other.

"You two," I said, "seem very lovey-dovey."

"We are," said Andrew. "Aren't we, Lou?"

"We are," replied Louise, "though how long it'll continue if you call me Lou, I can't tell." She leaned forward and whispered in my ear, "I've gone off Matt."

"That's lucky," I whispered back. "No one gets hurt."

"Except Matt." Louise giggled.

"He doesn't look hurt." Matt, on the other side of the room, seemed closely wound around a dark young lady I'd never seen before.

"That's Rosie. First reserve." Louise giggled again. "I've had too much punch. I'd better stop."

All at once I felt overwhelmingly tired and depressed. The steam and cigarette smoke were stinging my eyes.

"I want to go home, Mike. Do you mind?"

"No. I was just thinking I'd like to get some air."

We said good-bye to everyone (which took twenty minutes) and left the Capricorn.

"All the buses have stopped running," said Mike. "Shall we get a taxi?"

"No," I said, "let's walk."

"It's over two miles," Mike said. "Aren't you exhausted?"

"Not that sort of exhausted. Come on."

We walked through the silent night streets of the city. We didn't speak a lot, beyond marveling that his mother had managed to get to the theater. I mentioned that my mother had said she'd seen Clare.

161

"We can go past her house," said Mike. "See if she's there."

"If she is, she's most likely asleep by now. It's one o'clock."

"She might not be."

Mike was right. As we walked past Hansel and Gretel's cottage, we could see Clare's light, high up near the roof, shining out over the black sea of trees under her window, greening the edges of the nearest leaves where it fell. She was back.

"I'll go and see her tomorrow," I said as we stood beside my gate.

"Mel," Mike whispered.

"Yes?"

"We will see each other when this is all over, won't we?"

"If you want to."

"I want to."

"So do I."

"That's OK, then."

"Yes," I said. "And anyway, it's not all over yet, is it? There's still three more performances."

"I know," said Mike, "but I feel as if it's getting ready to be over, now the first night's gone, know what I mean?"

I nodded. I knew exactly. It was Time (blast it!) doing its you're-having-a-marvelous-time-so-I'll-speed-up routine. "It's up to us to enjoy every minute, then," I said, "and then hang on to the memories as hard as ever we can."

"Right. Good night, Mel."

" 'Night."

He looked all around our street before he kissed me, to make sure lights were out in upstairs windows. I was glad my mother's window faced the back. She was bound to be awake. As I let myself in quietly the thought occurred to me: I wouldn't put it past her to come and have a peek through the front-room curtains. It was just the sort of thing she would do. I listened in the hall for guilty foot-steps tiptoeing across the landing, but I heard nothing so I took off my shoes and crept up to my room.

In the movies, Our Star lies back in a foam of lacy pillows, wearing a satin nightgown that most people would give their eyeteeth to be able to wear to a ball, and the Hero in a silk dressing gown sits at the bottom of the bed reading her tidbits from the many newspaper reviews. Every tidbit confirms that she is Wonderful, and has every right to satin nightgowns, lace pillows, and a silk-clad Hero. My awakening was not quite like that, though I *did* get a tidbit, or what my mother called A Mention.

I opened my eyes in a tangle of rumpled quilt to hear my mother, who was bouncing around the room in a manner more suited to a toddler, shouting: "Mel, wake up! Quick, you're in the paper. You've got a mention. There's a review. In *The Guardian*."

I blinked. I thought: nothing much can have been going on last night, down in London. "Read it to me," I said. "Slowly."

"Right." My mother sat on the floor and started to declaim. " 'Project Theater's *Three Sisters* with a cast made up entirely of young people was a brave attempt to bring new shades of meaning to the text. The play may have lost certain nuances from the youth and relative inexperience of the players, but this was more than made up for by a sense of freshness and of something newly discovered. It is invidious in productions like this to pick out individual performances, but I did feel that Dinah McLaren made a most beautiful and innocent Irina, Louise Flynn and Mike Corderly a suitably anguished and tormented Masha and Vershinin, and Mel Herbert a deliciously overbearing and vulgar Natasha. Chris Taverner directed this delightful production, and he was well served by Clare Bradshaw's simple but effective sets.' There."

"Deliciously overbearing and vulgar," I said. "Me. I've actually got my name in *The Guardian!* I'm famous!" I leapt out of the bed and did a dance around the room, for all the world as if my polyester nightie had just turned to satin.

After breakfast I telephoned everyone I could think of, and we *ooohed* and *aahed* and quoted the review at one another, over and over again. By eleven o'clock I knew the thing by heart. It was like one of those tunes that repeat and repeat themselves, running around in your head until you feel you're going mad.

After lunch, I went to visit Clare.

"Go up," said Mrs. Sandler. "I'm sure she'll be happy to see you." I wasn't so sure, but I went up anyway.

"Mel!" said Clare. "How lovely to see you! Come in. Have you seen *The Guardian?*"

"When I die," I said, "the words 'a deliciously overbearing and vulgar Natasha' will be found engraved upon my heart. And," I added, "he appreciated how good the sets were. Clearly a man of tremendous discernment."

"Have a cup of coffee." Clare laughed.

"I will, but I want to know first—did you see it?"

"Yes, I saw it. Joyce let me creep in at the back. I don't think anyone saw me."

"By anyone I suppose you mean Chris. Other people saw you. My mother saw you."

"Well, it doesn't matter. I saw it and it was great. I was quite surprised, really, at how good it was."

"Did you cry?"

"Of course."

"That's always a good test. It must be OK if you cry."

"Rubbish. I cry at everything. It means nothing at all . . ."

I said: "I made friends with Dinah last night, you know. She asked me to. I'd had a row with her before . . . about you and Chris . . . and her and Chris . . . and even last night when I said we were friends, I told her again that I thought what she did was awful. I do think it was."

"You're sweet, Mel."

"Don't make it sound as if I'm about seven, Clare. It just so happens that I think Dinah is selfish. About a lot of things."

"She's also very beautiful."

"That's no excuse."

"I know it isn't. I'm just pointing it out."

"What're you going to do, Clare? Are you doing *Othello*?"

"Yes, I've got to do that. I promised. But then I'm leaving. I've got a job with a theater company based in Glasgow, starting in January."

"Then you're going away?" Much of the happiness I'd been feeling fell away.

"Not till after Christmas."

"I still wish you weren't."

"It's not Australia, you know. You *can* come and visit me."

"Really?"

"Yes, of course. Why not?"

"Great. I will. Thanks. You made me feel quite sad for a while."

"Nonsense," said Clare, "you've everything to be happy about. Now tell me every single thing that's happened since I left."

Scarcely have the plaudits of the first-night crowd died away, scarcely has the ink dried on all the rave reviews (there were two more in local papers), when lo and behold, you are in the auditorium for NOTES, which is simply another name for a POST MORTEM. To listen to Chris, just before we went on for the second night of the show, you'd think we hadn't put a foot right, any one of us. This was too quick and that too slow. A was in the wrong place, B was blocking C, D had her back turned to the audience, E forgot to put a certain prop in its right place. No less than eight lighting cues were slow, certain persons took longer than they need have done getting on and off the stage—the long and the short of it was: however marvelous we may all have been (and we *had* been, Chris said, make no mistake about that), we were all perfectly capable of being at least fifty percent better tonight.

"So," he said, "off you go and dress. It's nearly the half already. And make sure you sock it to them tonight."

We socked it to them that night and the next, and by the time the last night arrived we felt like old hands. Coming in for the last show, I was reminded yet again of school:

the last day of the school year. Soon, we'd all be leaving the self-contained world we'd made in this building, going back to join the other worlds in which we lived our normal lives. As soon as I reached the theater I thought: this is the last time I shall . . . and I went on thinking it. The last time I shall:

— greet George.

— open my dressing-room door and hang my coat on the back of it.

— say hello to Ruby, Dinah, Louise, Tricia, Ruth, Chris, Janet, Ruby, Mrs. McLaren.

— hear the half being called.

— put on this green belt.

— wear these clothes.

— walk onto this stage.

— kiss Matt.

— see Mike kissing Dinah.

— look at the avenue of firs.

— hear all the applause.

The dressing room had a look of home about it, even after such a short time. I didn't want to leave it. Once, the room had appeared featureless and cold to me, but now, with our gowns on the backs of the chairs, our good-luck cards curling at the corners from the hot glare of the naked bulbs, our makeup towels, and deodorant sprays, it seemed to embrace me as I went in, to fall around my shoulders like a comfortable shawl. I looked around it for a long time, willing myself to remember it like this, not as it was going to be in about three hours, stripped of life, stripped of all of us, back to being an empty room. Grayish walls and the marks of spilled powder on the Formica dressing table surface. Empty costume rails. Blank mirrors. All the lights turned off.

By the time we'd taken our last curtain call (our sixth) I was in tears. So was almost everyone else, although the boys (silly things!) chewed their lips, blinked their eyes, and pretended to be frightfully manly and not a bit upset really.

Our dressing room was loud with sniffing and nose blowing. We threw the flowers (long since faded) into black plastic bags provided by George. We gathered our harvests of cards, notes and telegrams, and put them away. We wrapped up boxes of chocolates for all the stage staff. We packed up our makeup and wondered when we would need it again, and worst of all, saddest of all, we watched the Prozorovs and their friends, their house, their world, all the words they'd spoken, all the emotions they'd felt, curl into the air like smoke and disappear as we went through each scene for the last time. It was exactly like walking along a road, through a landscape which you were convinced was real, only to discover that it was rolling itself up behind you like a carpet, leaving bare floorboards where it had once been.

Dinah and I were the last ones left in the dressing room at the end. She had already changed and was staring into the mirror. I was being deliberately slow. I thought of the first time Dinah and I had been together in an empty dressing room, and felt vaguely annoyed.

"If this were a story," I said, and didn't realize I'd said it aloud until Dinah turned to me and said:

"Sorry, were you talking to me?"

"Not really. Just wittering on."

"What about?"

"You."

"Me?"

"Yes. I was just thinking that if this were a story, you should have got your comeuppance."

"What for?"

"You know damn well what for."

"What sort of comeuppance? Chris leaving me at the end, realizing what a fool he's been all along, it's really Clare he loves, etc., etc. Something along those lines, were you thinking of?"

"I suppose so . . . or some dreadful revenge . . . like being truly awful in the play . . . but you were good. I'd like you to know that whatever else you've done, I *did* think your Irina was lovely."

"Ta ever so. And as for the rest, well you know it doesn't work like that, with people getting their comeuppance, as you put it."

I nodded and said nothing. Privately, I was thinking what a pity this was. A sadistic impulse made me imagine Dinah behind the counter of the mouse sweetshop, but the picture faded almost before I'd thought it. Dinah was clearly destined for another kind of life. As though she'd been reading my mind, she said:

"I'm leaving home after Christmas, you know. I'll be eighteen by then. I'll move into Chris's flat." She smiled. "If you want to get in touch ever."

"Right," I said.

Dinah stood up. " 'Bye, then, Mel."

"Cheerio. See you." She was gone. Who knew if I would see her? Other than on stage, being strangled as Desdemona. I blinked tears away from my eyes, thinking of Mummy Mouse alone in Dinah's white bedroom, looking at where the cuttings had been pulled away from the paintwork, rattling skeletal hangers in empty cupboards, and wondering where it was exactly, that other world that Dinah had found.

I stood up to leave. Don't look back, I thought. Turn the light out. Go out of the room and that's that.

"I'm off, George," I said, when I reached his cubbyhole. "Thanks for everything."

George put his newspaper down and looked at me solemnly.

"Miss Mel, good-bye and good night to you. I hope it won't be long before we see you here again."

"I hope so, too. It's been . . ." I couldn't think of how to put it.

"It's been a revelation," said George. That wasn't quite the way I would have phrased it, but there you go. "I said it'd be trouble, casting all of you lot in Chekhov . . . well, I'm not someone who can't admit when I've been wrong. No, you all did him proud. Chekhov, I mean. Yes. I was bowled over. There." He relaxed with an air of someone getting a difficult confession off his chest.

"Thanks, George," I said, "and good night."

" 'Night, miss," he nodded and took up his newspaper again.

That was six weeks ago on the Saturday night. On the Sunday, I watched them striking the set. On the Monday, I broke my ankle. I'd arranged to meet Mike outside the theater, and I'd arrived there before him. The wall running along the edge of the wasteland was quite a decent size now: quite high and going along in a businesslike way for about ten meters. There was no one around, and I couldn't resist it.

"Ladies and gentlemen," I said to myself, "you are about to witness the most spectacular feat in the field of tightrope walking since last Tuesday. The great, the fantastic, the one and only . . ." I was walking along the wall by now, pointing one foot in front of the other, holding my arms

171

out gracefully, when all at once I slipped (I'll never know how—perhaps it was the fault of the wall) and fell heavily onto my ankle. By the time Mike arrived, I was weeping with pain and rage. He ran into the theater and telephoned for an ambulance, and then he came and sat on the ground with his arms around me.

"I've rung your mother," he said. "She'll meet us at the hospital."

"She'll kill me." I started crying again.

"No, she won't," Mike said. "Of course she won't. You'll be fine. I'm coming with you in the ambulance. With any luck they'll put the siren on." I could tell he was quite looking forward to the ride. I closed my eyes and leaned against him, waiting for the ambulance.

This book, with the melted ice-cream covers, is almost finished. Over the page I can see Clare's message. I suppose I have to agree with it—there must be lots of small happy endings: perhaps that's what it means. Not one glorious final curtain followed by rapturous applause and then darkness, but a series of beginnings and endings of all shapes and sizes. I began writing in this book and I've nearly finished. *Three Sisters* ended and, lying on my bed, began. I was confined to my island, looking out of the window at the open sea. Soon, that will be over too. There's a very menacing pair of crutches leaning against the wall. I'm still not allowed to put my foot on the floor, but I can hop about here and there, more and more each day. Mike comes to help me. He laughs instead of doing anything constructive, but I'll get the hang of these crutches if it's the last thing I do.

I miss the constant company of a lot of people. I even want to go back to school sometimes. That, in the end, was the best part of being in *Three Sisters*: being so close to so many people. They come and visit me. Even Dinah has been, with offerings from the mouse-sweetshop. They come in ones and twos, and it's not the same. Without the play to hold us together, we find less and less to say to one another. There's every likelihood that this time next year, Mike and Clare will be the only people I'm still seeing. But (Clare's handwriting is rebuking me from the bottom of the page), I can do it all again. A different play, and different people, but nevertheless, a show. How's this for a happy thought, Clare? Bertolt? ONE PRODUCTION CLOSES, ANOTHER GOES INTO REHEARSAL. It's almost enough to make a person throw her crutches to the four winds and break into Theatrical Cliché Number Ten: a fast chorus of "There's no business like show business." OK, Maestro, take it from the top and give it all you've got. Yeah!

"There must be happy endings: must, must, must!"

Bertolt Brecht: The Good Woman of Szechwan.